BETTER LEFT BURIED

When your life is in danger, who do you really want on your side? Someone good, someone decent, someone who only ever does the right thing?

Couldn't the opposite be true? What if, when your world grows dark, you're better off with someone who's lived in the shadows? Someone who's seen and done things you can't even imagine. Someone who's prepared to do whatever it takes.

Maybe, when your life threatens to collapse beneath you, the only person who can help is the last person on earth you should actually trust.

BETTER LEFT BURIED

Emma Haughton

USBORNE

To James, Hetty, Chip, Flan and Josh

First published in the UK in 2015 by Usborne Publishing Ltd., Usborne House, 83-85 Saffron Hill, London EC1N 8RT, England. www.usborne.com

A CIP catalogue record for this book is available from the British Library.

J MAMJJASOND/15 ISBN 9781409566700 03155/1 Printed in the UK.

PROLOGUE

When it happens, I'm so lost in my thoughts I barely notice. A yank on the steering wheel and we spin into a U-turn, heading back up the road the way we came. I peer into my side mirror. Right behind us a large black car does the same manoeuvre.

My blood goes cold. Oh god…oh shit…it's true. They're really after us.

We're racing down the carriageway. I watch the needle of the speedometer steadily climbing…sixty…seventy… eighty, before we veer off into a side road, accelerating along a narrow lane through the forest, pine trees whizzing by perilously close. A sharp left and we're bouncing over a mud track. Things tumble around the car, and I grab the handle above my door to keep my balance.

"Hold on!"

The man hauls on the steering wheel again and all at once we're in among the trees. The suspension groans as we hit a small rock and he swerves to avoid a stump. We come to a halt in a mass of moss and ferns.

"Stay here!" he barks, leaning over and sliding an arm under his seat. Fiddling with something, like it's stuck.

"Damn!" He twists himself round so he can reach even further.

A faint ripping sound, and his hand emerges holding a fat brown envelope with duct tape hanging from each side.

What the... I don't even get to finish the thought before he rips it open and my breath freezes in my throat as I glimpse cold grey metal.

A gun.

He's got a gun.

I yelp in shock. But before I can say anything, do anything, think anything, he's out the car and running through the trees.

I sit there, whimpering, my breathing jagged with fear and dread. I sit there and it's as if time is suspended. No time at all and all the time in the world passes before I hear the shot.

And the silence that follows.

I keep perfectly still, too frightened to move or scream or cry, and wait for whatever will happen to happen. Until it feels as if that's all I've ever been doing, just sitting here, waiting for it all to end.

"Not bad, Sarah."

Mrs Perry inclines her head as I sing the closing bars of the Bach, then lifts her hands from the piano keys and turns to face me. "A little wobbly in parts, especially around the adagio."

She pauses, waiting for my response.

"I'm sorry." I shift the weight on my feet. "I'm a bit tired today."

"Right." Mrs Perry gives me one of her searching looks. "I can see that, Sarah. And this is a challenging piece. Well within your capabilities, yes, but if you're going to be ready, you'll have to work much harder on it."

I nod, picking up my score from the music stand and putting it back in my bag. "I promise I'll practise more this week."

She smiles as she stands. "Remember those breathing exercises I showed you. And your posture, Sarah. You still need to focus on your posture." Mrs Perry places one hand on her belly and lifts her chin; instantly her whole body seems taller.

"Okay." I bite the inside of my lip, trying not to show that I'm upset. Or how exhausted I really am.

It doesn't work. Mrs Perry walks over, taking both my hands in hers, and looks me full in the face. I get a faint tinge of perfume, something light and floral.

"Sarah, I hope you don't feel I'm being too hard on you."

"I don't, I—"

"You're so talented, and I know you can do this. But even with a voice as lovely as yours, you need to be well prepared. In a top-level audition like this, they're looking for excellent technique as well as raw talent."

She squeezes my hands gently, then takes a step back to get me in full view.

"Are you eating properly?"

I clear my throat. "Yes."

"Seriously, Sarah, every week there seems to be less of you." She frowns. "You're not on a diet, are you?"

"No," I say quickly, withdrawing my hands from hers and grabbing my bag. "Really. I…" I can't think how to explain. That after everything that's happened, food is somehow the last thing on my mind.

Mrs Perry gives me another questioning look. "So how are things at home?"

"Fine," I lie, taking a deep breath and forcing myself to appear brighter. "Better, I mean. Mum's doing better, I think."

Mrs Perry sighs. Puts her hand on my arm. "I'm concerned, Sarah, that's all. Worried this is getting too much for you…so soon after…"

She doesn't say it. Thank god.

"I'm okay," I say, more firmly than I intend. "I just want to get on…you know, keep going."

I can't bear the sympathy in her eyes any longer, so pull the money out of my purse and leave it on top of the piano.

"I'll see you next week," I say and dash out of the room, almost tripping over the cat in the hallway.

I know there's nothing in the fridge at home, so I call in at the corner shop on the way back. Pick up four packs of sliced bread, three tins of baked beans, a few apples and some mild Cheddar. And more butter. The one thing Mum will always eat is buttered toast – she must be just about made of the stuff by now.

But she might have a cheese sandwich. Maybe an apple if I cut one up.

I'm queuing at the till when I spot a girl with long blonde hair over by the fruit and veg, laughing into her mobile phone. Abigail Turner.

"Oh god," I mutter under my breath. I haven't seen her since summer term ended three weeks ago – and I don't want to see her now.

But it's too late. She's already spotted me.

"Hey, Sarah!" Abigail raises her hand and smiles. She says something into her phone, then pops it into her bag and heads in my direction.

"Hi! It's *so* good to bump into you." Her voice too bright for it possibly to be true. "How are you?"

"Hi, Abby. I'm fine, thanks. And you?"

"Oh, you know. Great. *Fabuloouuus*," she drawls, stretching out the word like elastic. "I'm going up to Edinburgh with Jonas next week, then we're off to Ibiza. You know, do all the clubs and beaches and stuff." She beams at me and does a funny little shiver. "I'm *so* excited!"

I can tell she's nervous. One of those people who smothers embarrassment by being extra bubbly. I try not to hold it against her.

"Wow! That's an awful lot of bread." She nods at the loaves crammed into the basket.

I muster a smile, trying to think of a polite exit. I'm sure Abigail is finding this as awkward as I am, and I need to get home and check Mum hasn't actually fallen into a coma or something.

"Just stocking up the freezer." I keep the smile fixed on my face in a way I'm hoping she'll start to find off-putting.

"Right." Abigail tucks a loose strand of hair back behind her ear with a nervous giggle. She's clearly struggling to think what else to say, and I almost feel sorry for her. She's making an effort, I remind myself; she could simply have pretended not to notice me and run away.

After all, Abigail wouldn't be the first. Since my brother died six weeks ago – barely a month after his twenty-first birthday – everyone at college seems to divide into two camps: those who go out of their way to avoid me, and those who go out of their way to show me how much they care.

Abigail falls in the latter. Six months ago she and I would hardly have exchanged a word if we'd bumped into each other like this. It's not as if we're actually friends or anything. Not like me and Lizzie.

But ever since it happened, since Max died, she's one of those people who seizes every opportunity to be nice.

I guess I should be grateful. Instead, it makes me want to scream.

"Hey," Abigail says suddenly, "I'm having a party when I get back. You know, to celebrate getting our exam results. Tanya and Zoë are coming – they're mates of yours, aren't they?"

I nod, though in truth I've barely seen them for weeks. I've hardly seen anyone except Lizzie since it all happened. I haven't exactly been feeling sociable.

"I'll try to make it." I shuffle forwards as the person in front of me pays and moves away. "Better go." I give Abigail what I hope is an appreciative look. "Have a nice summer."

"And you!" she says, beaming, as I turn to face the cashier.

It's hot, even for August. I'm sweating by the time I get to Foxton Road, and my arms feel like they might fall off. I stop for a minute, put down the shopping. Shake some life into my fingers, then slip off my rucksack and open it up, stuffing the apples and cheese and one of the loaves inside. I struggle to zip it up again and heave the bag back onto my shoulders.

As I straighten, I see this guy heading towards me, walking quickly, one hand thrust into the pocket of his jeans, the other punching on his mobile with his thumb.

We're both near the point where the pavement narrows between the postbox and one of those tall silvery trees, the kind with peeling bark and a fat, knobbly base. There's barely enough room for two people, let alone one hampered with shopping bags, so I pause to allow him past. He doesn't notice me waiting. He's too busy reading something on his phone.

He looks sort of familiar, though I'm pretty sure we've never met. I shudder. Oh god, please don't let it be one of my brother's friends – it's more than I can bear right now.

I edge between the two cars parked beside me, intending to cross to the other side of the road. It's a tight squeeze, and as I heave one of the bags over the front of the nearest car, the corner of the plastic catches on the wing mirror. A tin of beans spills out, bouncing off the bonnet and onto the ground, rolling under the bumper.

Damn. I bend down to retrieve it, hoping I haven't damaged the paintwork. When I get up, the man is only a metre or two away.

His gaze fixes on mine. For a second he stares at me blankly, nothing registering in his features. I'm still not sure I recognize him, though his face is hardly the kind you'd forget. Lean and angular, with the lightest grey eyes, gazing at me with an intensity that's almost startling.

But if anyone is startled, it's him. His blank expression tightens into shock. He stops dead, and I take in the black hair, the leather jacket and dark-dyed jeans. And the twitch in his left eye; a rapid, blinking motion like a kind of tic. He doesn't move, just looks at me as if I'm the last person in the world he ever expected to see.

The last person in the world he ever *wanted* to see.

I feel my cheeks flush. What on earth is this guy playing at? Why is he gawping at me like that?

I open my mouth to speak, but he beats me to it.

"Shit," he says under his breath, then suddenly he's gone. Turns on his heels and starts walking back the way he came, only quicker, as if he can't get away fast enough. I'm so stunned that I just stand there, watching, until he darts into Cambourne Avenue and disappears out of my sight.

sunday 7th august

Lizzie's sitting on my bed, skimming through a magazine. Not reading, but flicking, as if she can't actually be bothered with any of it. Her long, wavy hair drooping over her face, her fingers restless, curling the corners of each page.

I'm lounging on a cushion on the floor, my back against the wardrobe door, trying not to let this upset me. With both of us working full-time over the summer, I can't help thinking we should be doing something decent with our day off, rather than moping around in my room. Especially when I could – *should* – be practising my singing.

Another lurch in my stomach at the thought of my audition in a little over a month. I push it away. "Hey, why don't we go into town? See what's going on?" I suggest, in my breeziest, most upbeat voice.

Lizzie doesn't even raise her eyes. Just screws up her lips to show she's not keen.

"C'mon, the sun's out. We should make the most of it. You know, before it starts raining again."

She yawns. "I'm not fussed, to be honest."

I feel my mood sink further. Surely Lizzie should be

cheering me up, not the other way round? If I can make an effort, why can't she?

Not that I'm complaining. Not really. In those first days after we got the news about Max, I couldn't have asked for a better friend. Lizzie was the one who rushed over and held me as I sat on my bed, too stunned to do anything. It was Lizzie who made me endless cups of tea and force-fed me slices of toast and pizza, and Lizzie who made sure I made it to my last few exams.

Lizzie cried with me. Lizzie cried almost as much as me.

It's only now, six weeks later, as I recover from those first shock waves of grief, that I can see my friend more clearly. Something's up with her, and has been for a while. Even before Max died, Lizzie had changed, I remember; all her energy and sparkle turned moody and listless.

I inhale, vetoing the urge to ask her again what's wrong. Every time I do she says she's fine. Sometimes, for a while, she acts all lively and breezy for my sake, but it's obvious she's faking.

"How's work?" I venture, trying a different tack.

She sniffs and briefly lifts her eyes to mine. "Okay."

"Sick of all the free stuff yet?" Lizzie's summer job is at the bakery on Townsend Street and she gets the pick of the leftovers at the end of the day.

She pulls a face. "Mum's in seventh heaven – she's going to end up as fat as a pig."

I grin. "More likely Toby will."

Lizzie manages a smile at the mention of her little

brother, then lapses back into silence. Flicks a few more pages of her magazine, her expression as blank as the models' inside.

Only when there's a beep from her phone does she show any sign of life. She grabs it, reading the message, her face contracting with concentration.

I'm about to ask who it's from when I hear a creak from the bedroom next door. Mum, in Max's room again. Ever since the police turned up on our doorstep, her existence has shrunk to this house – more specifically, my brother's bedroom. Mum spends half her time in there now, amongst his books and magazines, the cupboards full of old games and stuff from when he was a kid.

Just sitting, staring. Trying to make sense of it all, I guess.

"*Shit*. My battery died." Lizzie glares at her phone, shoves it back into her pocket.

"Anyone important?'

"Only my mum." She says it too quickly, her eyes darting away from mine, and I realize I don't believe her. But why would she lie?

I gaze at her, wondering whether to pursue it. Decide against it.

"Hey, you picked where you want to go yet?" I ask to change the subject. "To uni, I mean."

Lizzie looks at me like that's the furthest thing from her mind. Though she must be thinking about it. Lizzie's wanted to study journalism since she got a piece into the school magazine – and university applications have to be in soon.

"How about we get these exam results out the way first?" she says, in a way that makes it clear she'd rather I dropped the subject. "Besides, *you* don't need to worry – you're all sorted."

Her tone sounds almost resentful, though I can't imagine why. Lizzie knows I have my heart set on going to the Royal Music School, which has the best reputation and the most intensive vocal course. But everything depends on my audition – flunk that and it's game over.

At least Lizzie has options.

I suck in my lips and try to pick something less touchy. "So, how about your big day? You thought any more about what you want to do?"

Lizzie stops leafing through the magazine, her face blank.

"Your eighteenth," I remind her. "It's only three weeks off."

"I dunno," she mutters. "Nothing much."

"A party?"

Lizzie shakes her head. "Too much hassle."

I frown. Too much hassle? This time last year Lizzie was planning the biggest bash ever for her eighteenth. Christ, at one point she wanted a whole crowd of us to go to Ibiza – her, me, Tanya, Zoë, Roo and Tabitha.

What happened to that Ibiza plan? I wonder. Lizzie just stopped mentioning it. I assumed it was because of me, because of what happened with Max.

But now I'm not so sure.

"So what do you want to do then?" I persist, refusing to let the matter drop.

Lizzie lifts her mouth in a kind of shrug. "I don't know. I haven't really given it a lot of thought. Not much, probably."

"Come on," I say, perplexed. "You can't be serious. It's your eighteenth, for god's sake. You can't just do *nothing*."

Lizzie shrugs again, a proper one this time, using her shoulders. "I can't think of much I want to do." She keeps her eyes fixed on her magazine, ignoring me.

What's got into her? I ask myself for the thousandth time. It's as if she's slipped away into some parallel universe, leaving the husk of my best friend. I mean, Lizzie was the original party animal, always the last girl standing wherever we went. The kind who was *never* short of an excuse to go out.

And as the oldest in our college year, Lizzie's the first to hit eighteen at the beginning of September. Everyone's expecting her to kick off our final year with a bang.

"Okay, you're right." She sighs and drops the magazine on the bed. "Maybe I should do something. Roo and Zoë keep on at me too. It's just that I don't feel like some mad celebration, that's all. Perhaps we could all go somewhere for a day? I could do with a break from this place."

"Where do you fancy?"

Lizzie thinks for a minute or two. "How about the beach or something? I haven't seen the sea in ages."

The beach. My mind flashes to that trip to Camber Sands when I was ten. "Coming to get you!" Max running towards me, grinning, a lump of seaweed in his hands, waving it in my face. Me trying to kick back at him as he laughs and dodges away.

"We could get the train down to Brighton," Lizzie suggests, her tone brighter. "The four of us. Go round the shops. Chloe Miller said there's some amazing little boutiques in the lanes off the seafront."

"Great." I push Max out my head and focus on my friend. "Sounds like a plan."

She seems genuinely into the idea. For a moment it's like having the old Lizzie back. The old Lizzie who was always up for everything.

"Right." She gazes back at me for a few seconds, as if she can't think of anything more to say. I realize I can't either and feel another pang of unease. Best friends since primary school and now we're having awkward silences?

"Hey, I forgot to mention," I say, anxious to fill the gap, "something really weird happened to me on the way back from my singing lesson."

"What?" Lizzie draws her knees up to her chest, hugging them with her arms. Finally giving me her full attention.

I tell her what happened a few days ago. "It was freaky. He just stared at me, then turned round and walked the other way."

She wrinkles up the end of her nose. "Why is that weird exactly?"

"I don't know. It just was. He saw me – I mean, he looked right at me – then suddenly did a U-turn and started off back down the road. But fast, as if he wanted to get away or something."

Lizzie's expression lifts into a grin. "Can you blame him?"

I pull a face at her. "Seriously. It was like he was running off."

"Maybe he forgot something and turned back? Or perhaps he was lost."

"But why would he look at me like that?"

"Like what?"

"So…kind of…intense. As if he recognized me. But he couldn't have done – I've never met him before."

"You sure?"

I hesitate. "I think so. At least, I'm sure I've never actually spoken to him, but he did look sort of familiar."

"Jeez, Sarah, I don't know." There's an edge to Lizzie's tone. As if she's tired of this whole conversation. "Why does it matter? Was he really hot or something?"

I stare at her for a second or two. "Forget it," I snap, dangerously close to tears. Why is she being like this? It's never felt this awkward, not in all the years we've been friends, since that first day I stood alone in the playground and she grabbed my hand and refused to let go till home time.

I blink as the gap in the conversation grows into a chasm, pressing my lips together in an effort not to cry.

"Oh god, Sarah, I'm sorry." Lizzie shuffles to the edge of the bed and lowers her head so it's level with mine. "C'mon, I apologize. I was only kidding." She kicks her foot gently against my arm so I'm forced to look up. "Honestly, don't get worked up about it. You probably just imagined it."

"I didn't!" My voice indignant now. "He—"

"I don't mean you made it up, Sarah…more you maybe got things a bit out of proportion. You know…because of Max." She sees my expression and backs off. "I only meant you've had a lot to deal with. It's bound to leave you a little edgy, that's all."

I sniff, my anger subsiding into doubt. Did he actually look at me that way? It's not as if I'm anything remarkable. Medium height, medium build, medium brown hair. Medium everything, really.

I rerun the whole scene in my head, fuzzier now. It was all so quick. Impossible to be sure what did happen. I can't picture the guy's face exactly so much as remember the way it made me feel.

Bewildered. Like there was something I was missing.

I give in and smile, letting go of my resentment. Lizzie's right. I'm making a big deal out of nothing.

After all, it's not as if I'm ever likely to see him again.

3

monday 8th august

I hear the sobbing the moment I get back from work. I drop my bag and race into the living room. Mum is sitting on the edge of the sofa, shoulders hunched, heaving slightly with each rush of tears.

A letter in her hands.

I sit beside her, put my arms round her waist and rest my head against hers. I don't say anything. I don't need to.

After a few minutes Mum straightens up. She folds the letter and drops it onto the coffee table, dragging the heel of her hand across her cheeks as she looks at me and tries to smile. I notice lines on her forehead and around her eyes that I swear weren't there a few weeks ago.

"I'm sorry, Sarah. I'm okay. Really. Just…you know."

Her gaze drops from mine, embarrassed. I'm almost relieved. I can hardly bear the pain I see there.

"I'm sorry," she says again. "I should have left it for your dad to open." She lifts a hand and smooths it over her hair. Her feet are bare and she's still wearing the T-shirt and pyjama bottoms she had on yesterday. There's a brownish stain on the right knee.

"Don't worry." I take the letter from her hand. "I'll deal with it."

"But…" Mum starts to protest, then sinks under the effort and gives me a grateful smile.

"Do you want a cup of tea?"

She nods. "Would you mind?"

As I wait for the kettle to boil, I hear her pad back upstairs and then the sound of the taps running in the bathroom. I unfold the letter.

It's from the university.

I scan through it. Signed by Mr Brian Thomas, the head librarian, it says Max's books are months overdue. Underneath is a list of maybe a dozen of them, with names like *Thermodynamics of Chemical Processes* and *Reaction Kinetics*.

Oh god. I guess no one told him what happened. I tuck the letter into the pocket of my jeans, and pour Mum's tea.

I force myself to go up to Max's bedroom. I hate coming in here. I hate even walking past on the way to the bathroom. My brother's room feels like a black hole in the heart of the house, sucking all the light, all the joy from our lives.

Like a memorial. Or a dirge, playing on a loop in the background.

I open the door to a rush of memories. And pain. There it all is. His books, his old laptop, that giant King Kong poster on the wall, the Warhammer figurines he used to play with. On the windowsill his collection of Rubik's cubes in different sizes, every one neatly solved. Everything in here a stabbing reminder, and somehow a reproach. Max – unbelievably – has gone, but his things remain. Abandoned. As if we've all turned our backs on him.

I close my eyes for a moment, pressing all the feelings down, and drag my attention to the books on the shelf. There's dozens of them, all the ones he used for his exams at school, and plenty more. Half my memories of my brother have a book in them.

I read each title carefully, comparing it with the list on the letter. Pick out a couple and throw them onto the bed. My heart contracts as I touch them. Max probably handled these that last week he was home; after all, he was holed up in here most of that time, only coming down for meals, leaving us wondering what was wrong. Had his final exams gone badly? Had he fallen out with someone?

"Just leave me alone, Sarah."

I'd opened the door to ask if he wanted anything from the shops. He was sitting in the chair, staring out the window as he said it.

"Leave me alone," he repeated.

So I did. I left him alone and the next day he'd gone. Without a word to anyone. We rang, left messages, but didn't worry much when he didn't return our calls – Max was always slack about stuff like that. We assumed he'd gone back to London, was busy finishing up at university.

But ten days later the police were standing on our doorstep.

Max had been found in our summer house in Sweden. His heart had stopped. That was all they could tell us. No one knew why. Nothing revealed at the post mortem, though we're still waiting for the inquest.

His heart just stopped. Dead.

A swoop of nausea. A picture in my mind, imagined, of my brother, lying naked on a cold, metal mortuary table.

Leave me alone, Sarah.

I shake away the image. Remember why I'm here. Check the list and scrutinize the bookshelves again, but I can't see any more. I go through the desk and the drawers, but there's no sign of them. They must be in the garage, in the boxes that came back from Max's room in London – no one's had the courage to deal with them since Dad dumped them in there several weeks ago.

"Sarah?" Mum's voice calls from the bathroom. "Are there any clean towels?"

I doubt it, I think, making a mental note to grab the pyjamas she was wearing and shove them in the wash. Hard to believe only a few weeks can reverse everything. That my lovely, busy, capable mother, who held down a full-time job running a local building society and yet still managed to make sure Max and I never went short of anything, can now barely run a bath without my help.

Her whole life undone by what no one can undo.

"I'll look," I call back, wondering how much more of

this I can take. Supporting her now is the least I can do, but sometimes it feels like I'm treading water, desperately trying to stay afloat while hidden currents drag me down.

As I turn to leave, I glimpse the back garden out of the window, the sprawling branches of the crab apple tree obscuring the end of the lawn. The flowers in the borders seem to glow in the warm evening light, not yet showing signs of their neglect, but the grass is now so long it's leaning over in places, flattened by the recent rain and wind.

An ache wells inside me. I always wanted this bedroom. Sometimes, when I was smaller and Max was out, I'd sneak in here and lie on his bed and stare across the garden to the ivy covering the back wall, wishing he would vanish so I could have it for myself.

And now I could, I realize, with a hot pang of guilt and sorrow. Max has gone and there's nothing to stop me moving in here any time I like. Dad wouldn't mind, and I doubt Mum has the strength to object.

Only now, of course, I no longer want to.

Max. I whisper his name under my breath and feel something bitter breaking through. None of this was his fault, I know that, but it doesn't help. No matter how much I miss my brother, I can't stop myself blaming him for leaving me stranded here. For the chaos his death has brought into our lives.

And for condemning me to spend the rest of mine being very careful what I wish for.

4

"I said NO!"

My eyes leap to the woman in front of me, my heart skipping in alarm. But her irritation is aimed at the small boy hanging on to the sleeve of her jacket, grizzling, his face crumpled and peevish.

I pick up the packet of chocolate biscuits and scan them, twisting the wrapper several times before the reader catches the barcode.

"Thomas, pack it in! I said you can have one when we get home."

The boy starts crying in earnest as his mother stuffs her shopping into bags with quick, jerky movements, her eyes hollow with exhaustion. As she pauses to slot her credit card into the machine, I let my eyes roam to the clock above the flower stand.

Half past two. One whole hour to go till break time.

To think I was actually excited at getting a summer job in the supermarket. My first proper job, if you don't count Dad paying me to help paint the spare bedroom.

But now every minute I spend here is a painful reminder

of what might await me if I flunk my audition. I'm not clever like Max…like Max was. I'm not university material. Without my music, my singing, I could be stuck doing this – or something like this – for the rest of my life.

Which would be okay if it was my choice. If I enjoyed it. But it's not, and I don't. All I ever wanted to do was sing. It's the only thing I know how to do well. Max got the brains; all I have is my voice.

The next customer, an older woman in a fuschia-pink coat, is already piling her shopping on the conveyor belt in precarious heaps. It jerks forward, and several bags of frozen peas start to avalanche. I jump up, grabbing them just before they hit the floor. As I sit back down I glimpse someone halfway up the newspaper aisle, over by the magazines.

A chill runs through me. I leap to my feet again, straining to see past the other customers.

There. A brief flash of dark hair by the greetings-card display. Black leather jacket, indigo denim jeans.

My breath dies in my throat. It's him. The guy I bumped into a week ago. I'm sure of it.

The pink-coat lady looks at me quizzically. "Is everything okay?"

"Excuse me!" I mutter. I slip out from behind the till and walk quickly up to the intersection by the cards, glancing around me.

No sign of him. What the hell?

"Sarah!" I turn to see Mrs Lucas, the supervisor, eyes widened into a furious question.

I spin about again, looking right along the aisles.

Nothing.

"Sarah!" Mrs Lucas's voice rises half an octave. I scarper back to my till, cheeks burning. "Sorry," I blurt. "I thought I saw someone drop their wallet."

Mrs Lucas frowns, staring up towards the card racks. Purses her lips and says nothing.

"I'm sorry," I repeat to the pink-coat lady, pulling out a wodge of plastic carriers. Notice my hand trembling as I try to separate them.

"You look as if you've seen a ghost," she says, her face crinkling into a kind expression.

I gaze at her helplessly, but she's already turned her attention back to her shopping. I grab the next item off the conveyor belt, trying surreptitiously to watch the checkouts and the exit as I work.

Still nothing. It's like he's completely vanished.

Or wasn't there at all, I think, as I help load the bags into the trolley. What was it Lizzie said before?

You probably just imagined it...Got things out of proportion.

She's right, I tell myself, feeling foolish. Max's death is obviously affecting me in ways I never realized. Making me paranoid. In that bereavement leaflet the doctor gave Mum, it said it was common to see the person that died for months, even years afterwards. Imagining you've glimpsed them in the street, that sort of thing.

It hasn't happened to me, though I kind of want it to. I'd like to see my brother again, even if it does mean I'm going a little bit crazy. When you miss someone that much, it's a trade-off you're happy to make.

But no Max. Nothing. Just an empty bedroom, and a mother who's fallen into a chasm of grief. A father who's barely coping himself.

Instead I'm seeing other kinds of ghosts. Inventing stuff where nothing's going on.

Going more than a little bit crazy.

5

wednesday 10th august

I get up at six the next day, determined to put in an hour or two of practice before work. But it's hard to sing when you're shivering. The shed is cold this early in the morning, dark clouds looming outside the window in mockery of summer. The mess of plant pots and garden tools, the half-used packets of seed and dried-out compost, all make my skin feel itchy and crawly.

I flip back to the beginning of the score, prop it up on Dad's old potting bench, and press play on my iPod dock. The sound of Mrs Perry's Schubert piano accompaniment fills the tiny space. A little tinny, but it's clear enough and I start again, this time sensing my mind and body loosen as I sink into the music, letting it pull me in until everything else drops away and there's just the swoop and soar of my voice above the piano.

I'm just reaching the end of the song when there's a knock on the shed door. I switch off the music, turn to see Dad standing there with a cup of tea.

"Morning," he says, putting it down on the bench in front of me. "Sorry to interrupt."

I shake my head. "I'm nearly finished."

"I heard you from the kitchen." He walks up and puts an arm round my shoulder, pulling me towards him so he can kiss the top of my forehead. "Lovely. Really haunting."

I smile.

"Sad," he says. "Your music always seems so melancholy these days. Lovely, but sad."

I look up at him in surprise. I guess he's right. I hadn't realized how much I'd been drawn to these pieces, their solemn, evocative beauty. Somehow, since Max died, I can't face anything more upbeat, more cheerful.

Dad releases me, examining the jumble inside the shed with a resigned expression. "I really should clear this place up. But why are you in here?"

"I needed to get in some practice, but didn't want to wake you."

A slight shift in Dad's posture. "I was awake anyway."

I don't ask why. I don't need to. Dad's maintained a flawlessly brave front since Max's death, but the dark shadows under his eyes reveal how much it has taken its toll. Not only the daily strain of coping with Mum and holding everything together. Dad had to fly to Sweden to deal with it all, returning home looking like he'd been to hell and back and barely survived the trip. And Dad had to clear Max's flat, since Rob, my brother's best friend and flatmate, wasn't around; didn't even bother to show up to the funeral, come to that.

"So," Dad says in a tone I know he's forcing into cheery. "Feeling confident?"

I pull a face. "Not exactly."

"When's the audition again?"

"Four weeks."

"You'll knock 'em out. They're bound to give you a scholarship. You've got the voice of an angel."

I smile, but don't answer. If only it were that easy. The more I practise, the more I discover how much I still need to do. Everything that's happened in the last couple of months has thrown me right off track; I'm always struggling to catch up.

"You're on the eight o'clock shift, aren't you?" Dad glances at his watch, then holds it up so I can see the dial.

I grimace at the time. "Yeah."

He goes to leave. Pauses. "I nearly forgot, could you pick up a prescription from the chemist? Mum was going to go, but she's got a headache."

"I'm on a double shift," I say. "But I'll call in at lunchtime."

Dad raises an eyebrow. I know he wasn't keen on me taking this job so soon after everything. I'm sure he'd prefer me to stay at home with Mum, though he's never actually said so.

God knows I'm tempted to chuck it in every moment I'm there, but with Mum on indefinite sick leave, our finances are stretched to the limit. More than that, my brother's death has left such a hole in our lives;

if I abandon my plans I'm scared I'll fall right in.

Like Mum.

"What's it for?" I ask. "The prescription."

"Just her antidepressants. And some more sleeping pills."

Again? I'm sure she had a new lot only a week or so ago. Didn't I read somewhere about sleeping pills being bad for you? Addictive?

Dad gives me a look that says everything. A look with a kind of despair in it, and I know we're both thinking the same thing. Is Mum ever going to recover from this?

As Dad shuts the shed door behind him, I pack up my music, trying to remember the stages of bereavement in that leaflet. Denial, depression, acceptance – something like that. Mum seemed to skip denial, sinking straight into depression with no sign of ever surfacing.

I'm beginning to think she needs more than another packet of pills.

I jog all the way to the bus stop. It starts to rain as I turn the corner of Guildford Rise – big fat raindrops, the kind you only get in summer. At the top of the road, the bus is already approaching. I up my pace to a sprint, reaching the stop just as it pulls in.

Standing behind the huddle of people waiting to get the bus, I try to catch my breath. My heart is pounding painfully and I feel sick and dizzy. Why? I wonder. I used to run long distance at school and never felt this bad.

Maybe I should have had breakfast. I meant to, but I was out of time. And appetite. I should make more of an effort – after all, skipping meals will hardly make me feel any better. And Mrs Perry is right; I need to keep my strength up.

I resolve to try harder as the bus door opens and a line of people files off. The woman in front of me shuffles forward and flashes her pass at the driver. I dig into my pocket for some change, about to hand it over when someone careers down the aisle, losing his balance as he bolts for the exit. He collides right into me, throwing me against the handrail.

"Steady on, mate," the driver yells after him.

The man turns and looks at me for a second, that wild tic in his eye. Then almost leaps off the bus.

Him.

This time there's no mistake. And from the way he slammed into me, no ghost either.

"He's dropped something." The driver leans over and stares at something on the floor by my feet.

I bend down and pick up the piece of paper. "Hey! You left this!" I yell, jumping onto the pavement and waving it in the air.

He doesn't turn round.

"HEY!" I shout more loudly, taking a few steps after him. "Wait! You've lost something."

A woman walking a fat little Dachshund gazes at me, but the dark-haired man keeps on going. Acting like he hasn't heard me.

"Forget it," the driver calls. "I've gotta go. I'm behind schedule as it is."

I stare up the road, wondering if I should run after him. But I'm late already and Mrs Lucas will be on the warpath. I hesitate, then get back on the bus.

"His loss, love," the driver says as I pay for my ticket. I find a seat at the back overlooking the street and peer out the window as we pull into the traffic.

Where is he?

As we pick up speed, I crane my neck to look back down the street. No sign of him, even though there's nothing on this part of Guildford Rise except terraced houses and the Methodist church. He must have doubled back, or crossed the road when I wasn't looking.

The bus turns off towards the town centre. I give up. Take a deep breath to try to calm my racing heart. Glance at the piece of paper I'm still clutching in my hand. Plain A4, the kind you use for printing, folded into half, then half again. I open it carefully, expecting a bill or official letter or something like that.

Instead there's a drawing, a network of lines in black biro, intersecting and joining up with one another. Every so often, seemingly random, an X. One with a circle around it. Altogether it makes a strange kind of pattern, like some complex game of noughts and crosses.

What the hell?

* * *

"What do you make of this?"

I hand Tony the piece of paper as he sits opposite, tray loaded with a greasy-looking pasty and a can of Coke.

"What's this?" He smirks. "A love letter?"

"You wish," I say, grinning because I know he's only teasing.

I like Tony. He's worked on the fish counter here for years, yet somehow manages to stay relentlessly cheerful. He was the one who showed me the ropes when I started, patiently explaining things even though I was clearly struggling to take it in with everything going on at home.

"Seriously, what is it?" He smooths the paper onto the table and peers at it through his glasses.

"No idea." I spent half my lunch break studying the weird diagram while waiting in the chemist for Mum's prescription, but still can't make any sense of it.

Tony spins the sheet around, seeing if turning it upside down will make it all fall into place.

Clearly not. He looks up and shrugs. "Interesting." He pulls the ring on his can and slugs back half of it. "Where'd you get this?"

"Someone dropped it on a bus."

Someone. My stomach gives another lurch of worry. Why do I keep seeing that guy? That encounter on the bus was…what? The third time in the last five days? Assuming that *was* him in the newspaper aisle yesterday, and not my imagination.

Who the hell is he? I wonder again. I still have the sense

I know him from somewhere, but for the life of me can't think where.

Tony rotates the paper again, studying it from every direction. I take another bite of my vegetarian lasagne. Wince at the bland rubbery taste and force it down.

"Hmmmm…" he says.

"What?"

"I reckon it's a map."

"Really?" I frown. "So what are those crosses?"

"Who knows? But this one," he points to a large upright cross on the intersection of two lines, "I'd say is a church. No idea what the others mean."

"But there's nothing written on it. No street names or anything. What kind of a map has only lines and crosses?"

"Dunno," says Tony. "It's a bit weird, I agree. But I came across something similar on a computer game once."

He traces a finger from one X to the next, following the shortest route through the lines. "Maybe it's so no one can read it. Only the person who made it. You've got to know what it's a map *of* before it makes any sense."

I swallow another bite of lasagne. Pick up the map. Tony's words make me feel odd somehow. There's something sinister about the whole thing. I'm tempted to just screw it up and bin it.

Instead I refold the paper and stuff it back into my pocket. "Anyway, my time's up. Back to the torture of the tills."

Tony leans back in his chair, lifting his feet onto my empty seat, and takes another long swig of his Coke. "Could be worse," he says, with a wink and a chuckle. "You could always be filleting fish."

6

wednesday 10th august

By the time I'm home it's getting dark. I let myself into a house full of silence. No sign of Mum and none of the downstairs lights are on. Dad must be working late again.

I creep upstairs and push open the door to their bedroom. Mum is asleep, her head pressed into the pillow. I put the pills I picked up from the chemist on her bedside cabinet then glance at the alarm clock.

Not even half past nine.

I watch her for a while, letting myself remember my other mother, my before-Max mother. The way she sat on the end of my bed each night to chat about my day. Coming to each recital, every concert, clapping so fast and loud I could pick out the sound in any round of applause.

Over on the windowsill I see the flowers Dad bought Mum are wilting, the stalks going mushy and brown. I go over to retrieve the vase, my eyes drawn to the fading light outside. I scan the street briefly, but there's nothing. Nothing but shadows in the dusk.

Calm down, I tell myself, still nervous and tense from

the earlier encounter on the bus. Could it have been coincidence? Seeing that guy so often? This is a small town, but not that small; it's not like you bump into people you know all the time.

And even if it was just chance, why behave so weirdly? Turning on his heels that first time he saw me. Ignoring me when I tried to give him back his map.

Again that nagging feeling that I recognize him from somewhere. But where? Not college, certainly. He's too old. Early twenties at least. Not any friend of Max's that I can remember. Nor any acquaintance of Mum or Dad.

"You're home late."

I spin round. Mum's pulling herself up in bed, her face smudged and bleary though she's not wearing any make-up. She hasn't worn any since the funeral.

]"I did a double shift," I say, giving her a smile.

"Have you had anything to eat?"

I shake my head. "I was going to make scrambled eggs."

"We could have them on toast. I picked up some more bread from the corner shop," she adds, as if she's achieved something monumental. Hard to believe that only a couple of months ago she was managing five members of staff.

As Mum turns on the lamp, I see her properly. My stomach tightens with anguish. She's been crying again.

"Did you have a good day at work?" She summons an unsteady smile.

"Great," I lie.

She looks relieved and I relax a little. Mum only wants

to know that I'm okay; give her too many details and she'll just find more to worry about.

"So you want some?" I ask. "Eggs, I mean."

Mum nods. "Please. I was going to get up and make myself a sandwich but…" She lets the sentence tail off, as if her lethargy doesn't need any explanation. One trip up the road and she's clearly exhausted.

"I'll bring it up." I give her what I hope is a cheery look and turn to close the curtains, vase still in my hand. It's then I spot something, at the exact moment the street lights flicker on, deepening the surrounding shadows.

There. Over by the postbox, what looks like a figure standing behind the lamp post. Gazing up at me.

The sound of glass shattering. A wet splash on my feet. I look down at the remnants of the vase, water pooling around it.

"Sarah?"

I glance back out the window. The figure has gone. The street is empty.

I run. Out the bedroom and down the stairs. Throw open the front door and sprint across the drive.

"Sarah?" I hear Mum calling after me. "What on earth's the matter?"

Even as I reach the pavement I can see no one is there.

"Sarah?" Mum's voice fainter now, like pianissimo on a piece of music. I take a few steps towards the street light, but fear lurches out of nowhere and stops me in my tracks.

"Get a grip!" I hiss to myself, curling my fingernails into my fists. *There's no one here. Whatever you thought you saw was all in your mind. There's nothing going on – bumping into that man again was only coincidence.*

I stand there, shivering, trying to make myself believe it. It doesn't work. I'm terrified. Overwhelmed.

"Sarah?" I turn around and see Mum is leaning out the bedroom window. "What's the matter?"

I just shake my head. "Nothing," I call up, feeling foolish. "Nothing at all."

When Mum's eaten and drifted back off to sleep, I lock myself in the bathroom, determined to calm down. I give the tub a good scrub before turning on the taps, and pour in some of the "relaxing" rose and jasmine bath foam Dad got me for Christmas. I strip off my T-shirt. Try to stuff it in the laundry, but the basket's full again.

I suppress a prickle of irritation. It's no big deal. I'll put a load on later.

As I slip off my jeans something falls out of my pocket. The strange map. I go to toss it into the bin, but change my mind. Unfold it instead, and have another look.

There's something familiar about this, I realize, with a lingering feeling of unease – it reminds me of something. I examine the patterns for a couple of minutes while the water cools, but still can't make any sense of them.

Who uses a map? I wonder. Everyone's got apps on their

phone. It's impossible to get lost these days, isn't it?

I give up. Leave the paper on top of the laundry basket as I inch into the bath, trying not to look at how thin my legs have become. I know what people think, that I'm deliberately starving myself, but I'm not. I don't want to be this skinny. It's more that food seems to have turned from something I once enjoyed into something that makes me feel sort of…weary. Even the idea of eating feels like a chore, another thing I have to do to keep going.

Sinking into the water, I inhale the flowery scent of the bubble bath and let the warmth banish the lingering presence of that figure in the shadows. *It was nothing*, I reassure myself. *There was no one there.*

But my mind is restless and jittery, and my anxiety resurges as I realize I forgot to do any practice. I let out a small moan of frustration. I meant to go right through the Purcell tonight, drilling myself on the trickier bits of phrasing, making sure my timing is exactly right.

Oh god. I promise myself I'll get up early again tomorrow and go back down to the shed. Squeeze in another hour before my shift starts.

Just four weeks till my audition. After years of working towards this, it seems impossibly close, and the thought makes my stomach clench again. My one opportunity to actually do something with my life, to do the only thing I really love, the only thing I'm any good at. And possibly my best chance to get away from this house, and the heaviness that's descended on us all.

But what if Dad's wrong? What if I don't walk a scholarship? What if I don't get in at all?

I grab the soap, smearing it over every inch of skin. I scrub it off with the rather grubby flannel hanging on the towel rail, then pour shampoo into my hand and lather up my hair.

I will get in, I tell myself firmly. I *have* to. There's no alternative. I'm not a brainbox like my brother.

Like my brother was.

Leave me alone, Sarah.

Max's voice echoes round my head, so real it's almost as if he actually spoke, and I suddenly wish more than anything that he was right here, right now, so I could talk to him, get all the answers we so desperately need. What was he doing by himself in Sweden when he died? And why didn't he tell us he was going?

But then Max was always secretive about his private life; even as a kid he'd never let you know where he'd been or who with. It's simply the way he was.

Sliding back down, I rinse my hair, letting it float around me. I close my eyes and try to clear my mind of its tangle of thoughts, but a picture of that map appears in my head, like an image burned on my retina.

Lines and crosses, intersecting and joining.

Somehow familiar.

Water sloshes over the side of the bath I sit up so fast, my heart beating a crescendo to the connection surfacing in my mind.

I dry my hands quickly on a towel and grab the piece of paper from the laundry bin. Orient it so the larger cross is in the top right-hand corner and study it carefully, checking off each line against the map in my head.

Oh god, I'm right. *I'm right.*

It *is* a map. Of here, of this town.

The big cross is St Stephen's church, and the line running beside it must be Winchester Road. I trace off Carrick Road with my finger, follow it along to the intersection with Graves Avenue, sliding it across to Hensham Green until my fingernail rests on the smaller X at the end.

My breath catches in my throat. I have to swallow before I can breathe.

X marks the spot. Lizzie's house. Or bloody close.

I trace the road back up to the other small X in the corner, feeling almost sick as I see it matches exactly. The supermarket where I work.

I glance at the third X. The one with the circle. This time I don't need to calculate where it is. I know from a single glance.

Our house.

I stare at the paper, the lines dancing and weaving as it begins to tremble in my hands.

7

"Go on, have a look."

I toss the map towards Lizzie and it lands in front of her on the picnic blanket.

She glances down, then carries on painting her toenails, sitting almost cross-legged and leaning forwards to reach her foot. "Wait a sec. What's the hurry?"

I chew the inside of my lip, listening to the buzz of insects on the flowers around us, watching her splodge a second layer of pink varnish across her big toe. It seems to take for ever. And she has another nine to go.

I lift my face to watch the clouds drifting across the sky. Thin, high summer clouds, not dense enough to block the heat from the sun. Birdsong in the trees in the neighbouring garden, sharp and sweet.

"Saraaaahhhhhhhhhhhhhhhhhh!"

Toby bursts out of the back door and dive bombs onto the lawn beside us, jogging Lizzie's hand. A gob of varnish lands on her ankle.

"Christ, Toby!" Lizzie glares at her brother, grabbing his arm and yanking him away. "Leave us alone, can't you?"

I ferret in my pocket and find a half-eaten packet of wine gums that's been lurking there since Dad last took me out for a driving lesson. Pick off a bit of fluff and chuck them towards him. Toby catches them with a deft swoop of his hand.

"Right. Now bugger off." Lizzie's harsh tone makes me wince. She never used to be so impatient with him.

The lack of reaction on Toby's face shows he's grown used to it. He retreats back into the house with a wrinkle of his nose that makes him look just like his sister, slamming the door behind him.

"For god's sake," Lizzie mutters under her breath.

"He's okay," I say, trying not to show my discomfort. Lizzie was always so great with her brother, especially after their dad cleared off three years ago. She was forever playing Lego and other games with Toby, taking him to the park to clamber all over the climbing frame, babysitting him while her mum was at work. Lots of the time we did it together.

"You only think that because you don't have to put up with him," she says, smearing more varnish across her toes. There's so much on the surrounding skin that her nails look crooked.

"Here, I'll do that." I gesture at her foot. "Have a look at this." I nod towards the map.

Lizzie sighs and hands me the bottle, spinning around so I can reach her foot. I screw the lid back on and give it a good shake. While she squints at the network of lines and crosses, I reapply the varnish in smooth, neat strokes, covering the bits she's missed or gone wonky.

"Okay, I give in. What is it? Some kind of puzzle?" Lizzie raises her head and looks at me.

"He dropped it. That guy."

"What guy?"

"You know, that man I told you about. The one who ran off when he saw me. He bumped into me on the bus yesterday and this fell out of his pocket." I don't mention last night's figure on the street. Even if there *was* someone hanging around, I don't know it was him.

Lizzie frowns. "So why didn't you give it back?"

"I did try, Lizzie. I got off the bus and called after him, but he acted like he hadn't heard me."

She twists the paper around, examining it. "How old was he, this guy?"

I shrug. "Early twenties, maybe?"

"What did he look like?"

"Dark hair. Slim. Really pale eyes. Kind of intense-looking."

Lizzie looks down at the map again. Studying it more closely now.

"At first I thought it was just some sort of drawing, a pattern or something," I say. "Then I showed it to Tony at work, and he figured it was a map." I finish her foot and beckon for the other one, leaning over to spin the sheet back so she's seeing it the right way.

"Look at it, Lizzie. That's St Stephen's church, and this

is Firth Street running off it. See?"

I trace the line to the X below. "This is my house, I reckon." Then I trace up ten streets or so to the other X. "This is pretty much where the supermarket is."

I complete the triangle at the final X. "And this is your road. It all fits."

Lizzie pulls her foot away, even though I haven't finished. She leans forward, staring intently at the paper, her finger touching the cross by her house. She doesn't say a word. Her eyes are sort of glazed and unfocused.

I wait for her to speak. She must be as puzzled by this as I am. What on earth is it all about?

But then Lizzie looks up at me and laughs. A shiny, brittle kind of laugh.

"Christ, Sarah, you really are getting paranoid, aren't you?" She tosses the map back at me and a breeze picks it up and blows it into the nearby flower bed. "Honestly, you could read anything into this."

I lean over to retrieve it and stare at her, dazed. "I don't think so, Lizzie. Look, if you count up the roads it matches exactly."

"I bet you could make it fit a thousand towns in England. They're all the same. It doesn't mean a thing."

There's something in her voice that isn't quite right. Her cheeks are flushed, and she's pressing her lips tight together. I know that expression. Whenever we had a sleepover and stayed up watching scary films, Lizzie would make this face when the tension got too much for her.

"He must live round here, though," I protest. "I mean, why else would I keep bumping into him all the time?"

Lizzie snorts. "You reckon he's stalking you or something? Come off it, Sarah. Don't be stupid."

I feel the heat rise to my cheeks. "I'm not being stupid, Lizzie. And I'm not imagining this, am I?" I fold up the map and hold it up in front of her face. "Or do you think I drew this myself, to get attention or whatever? Is that what you believe?"

I wait for her to deny it, but Lizzie holds my gaze with arched eyebrows. A hardness in her eyes I've never seen before. Something defensive, almost defiant. I stare at her for a few more seconds, then look away.

I don't understand anything about Lizzie's reaction. She's clearly rattled by what I've just shown her, so why pretend it's nothing? And why be so horrible about it?

I'm bewildered. I mean, it's not as if we haven't argued before, but it's never been like this. So tense…almost hostile. Even that time we fell out over the little silver cup we won for our junior science project, it didn't feel this precarious; a few days later we were laughing over the whole thing – and Lizzie let me keep the cup.

But this – this moodiness, this distance – has been going on for months. I can't for the life of me think of a reason for it, and I'm sick of asking and being fobbed off.

"Okay." I screw the cap back on the varnish bottle and drop it onto the picnic rug. "In that case, forget it."

I don't bother with goodbye, just grab my bag and leave

by the side gate, half expecting to hear her voice calling me back.

But there's nothing. Only the sound of Toby, somewhere in the house, turning up the volume on the TV.

8

friday 12th august

"Sarah?"

A hand on my shoulder. I give a little yelp of alarm and spin round to see Mrs Lucas – the supervisor – gazing at me.

"Are you okay?" she asks, looking concerned.

I nod. "Sorry. You caught me by surprise."

Mrs Lucas frowns. "I was wondering if you wanted another late shift on Saturday? Jonathan can't do it, something about his mum's birthday. Could you fill in for him?"

"Okay," I mumble. "No problem." Though truthfully the prospect of another eight hours in this place makes my heart sink.

Mrs Lucas looks me over again. "You sure you're all right? You look…well…rather peaky."

"I'm fine." I smooth down my uniform and try to appear more composed. "Really."

She gives me a brief smile and leaves me to finish stacking the row of biscuits. I take a deep breath, resisting the urge to check the aisle when she's gone.

He's not here, I repeat to myself silently. *He's not here.*

I never used to be like this. So nervous. Before Max died, I didn't worry much about stuff. I grew up assuming things would go well, that all you had to do was work hard and hope for the best. I was one of life's natural optimists.

But my brother's death was so sudden, so senseless, it's turned my world upside down. Made me see disaster round every corner.

And now I can't stop thinking about that guy. Can't shrug off the feeling that he *is* around here somewhere. Watching. Waiting. That map has me shaken. I mean, I might be overreacting. I might be imagining things. Maybe seeing him several times in a few days *was* a coincidence. But that map?

My house. Lizzie's house. The supermarket. What could it possibly mean?

I glance over my shoulder, still unnerved. Scan the shoppers milling around me. Most are women, one with a toddler slotted into the front of her trolley. A youngish man with a basket, browsing the crisps further up the aisle.

No sign of *him*.

Why? I ask myself, for the thousandth time, as I unload another box of biscuits. Why would anyone be following me?

And for the thousandth time I have no answer. I can't think of a single reason. It's ridiculous. Crazy. It's no wonder Lizzie reacted so badly.

Lizzie. My chest tightens as I remember yesterday.

She hasn't been in touch since, and that hurts. No way she didn't clock how upset I was. No way at all.

I think back to that night we heard about Max. A feeling in my heart like a bruise as I recall Lizzie's arms around me, holding me tight. *I'm sorry, Sarah. I'm so, so sorry.* Over and over she said it, like Max's death was something she could somehow have prevented.

Like it was *her* brother that died.

I'll ring her, I decide, folding up the cardboard box and stashing it at the back of the cage. Text her at least. I nearly did this morning, before I came in, but something held me back. Something about the way she looked at me just before I left. As if…as if right at that moment she couldn't stand being anywhere near me.

Stop it, I tell myself firmly, as I open another box of biscuits. *Stop being so bloody paranoid. Lizzie doesn't hate you. And there'll be some sort of rational explanation for all this.*

As I stack the digestives onto the shelf, I notice I've put the custard creams in the wrong slot. I sigh. Start again.

I'll talk to Dad, I resolve. Tonight, after I've been to Mrs Perry. I'll show him that piece of paper, tell him what happened and see what he thinks. If he says it's nothing to worry about, then I'll throw the thing away and put all of this out of my mind.

And I'll definitely call Lizzie.

*   *   *

When I get back from Mrs Perry's, Dad's already home. Squatting on his heels on the kitchen floor, searching through the food cupboard.

"Good lesson?" he asks, as I dump my music on the table.

I shrug. "Not bad." In truth I made a mess of the Strauss, never quite able to bring out the haunting beauty of the song. I could see Mrs Perry fighting to keep the disappointment from her expression.

"You're back early," I say, thinking this is a good omen. It will give us a chance to talk.

Dad looks up and smiles and I feel my heart lift a little. "I had a meeting over in Wandsworth. It wasn't worth returning to the office."

He shoves a few cans aside to get to one at the back. Picks out a tin of ravioli and sets it on the counter. "Actually, there's something I need to tell you, Sarah." He straightens up and fixes me with a serious expression and I feel a buzz of worry.

"Me too," I say quickly. "There's something I want to talk about as well."

"What?" Dad sounds immediately concerned.

"You go first."

He loosens his tie and exhales loudly, not quite meeting my gaze. "I've got to go away for a few days. Maybe a week. Up to Scotland." Picking up the ravioli, he checks the use-by date on the bottom. Chucks it in the bin.

"Scotland? Why?" My voice a good octave too high.

"There's a problem out on the rigs. I have to go up and sort it. No one else can."

"Right," I say, wondering how they'd cope if Dad had an accident or fell ill or something. I stare at his back as he moves his search to the fridge, my heart sinking in a slow kind of panic. He's so like Max, I can't help thinking – at least in some ways. Forever focused on what he's doing at that moment. Taking it for granted that everyone else is as strong as he is.

I wish I could say this to him, actually mention Max's name, but Dad's way of coping seems to be to pretend he never existed. So I keep quiet, but my silence clearly gives something away because Dad stops picking through the leftovers and looks right at me.

"Sarah, I'm sorry. I know it's bad timing, but I can't get out of it. Really."

I stare at him, wondering why I feel so churned up. I mean, it's hardly the first time he's been off on business. And it's only a week. Why does the idea fill me with panic?

Then I remember the last time Dad went away. When he flew out to Sweden to identify my brother's body.

My chest tightens as I recall the taxi arriving. Only me and Aunt Helen to see him off. Mum upstairs, slurry with the drugs the doctor prescribed to calm her down. Dad fixated on leaving; on doing whatever had to be done.

Possibly the worst day of my life.

I close my eyes briefly. Shut off the memory before it makes me cry. "When are you going?"

"Day after tomorrow. Got a mid-morning flight."

So soon. My heart swoops with panic. The thought of me and Mum, alone again, making me dizzy. Can she cope without him?

Can I?

"You'll manage, won't you, the pair of you?" asks Dad, reading my mind. Though my anxiety is probably written all over my face. "You'll be okay looking after Mum?"

Almost unimaginable that Dad would have to ask me that a few months ago. I'd have laughed. Mum was the one who managed everything – her job, the house, us – and still found time to go shopping with Aunt Helen or have lunch with her friends. Who went swimming three times a week, and even volunteered at the local cinema club every Wednesday evening.

Back then Mum could handle anything – just not the death of her only son.

"Sarah?"

I force myself to nod. "Sure, we'll be fine. Don't worry."

Dad looks relieved, and I realize he's more anxious about leaving than I thought. "Your turn," he says, leaning against the work counter and folding his arms.

"My turn for what?"

"You said you had something to tell me."

"It's nothing." I say it quickly, turning away so he can't read my expression. All at once I no longer feel like confiding in him. What's the point if he's not even going to be here? And even if he believed me – doubtful, given even

Lizzie thinks I'm bonkers – I don't want him fretting all the time he's gone.

"When are your exam results out?" he asks, making a guess at what's on my mind.

"Next week."

"Feeling confident?"

I shrug. I don't think I've done brilliantly – considering what happened in the middle of my exams – but with any luck I'll be okay.

Dad glances in the veg basket then abandons the hunt for something edible. "Pie and chips? I could go to the chippy over on Baker Street."

My stomach curdles at the thought, but I say yes anyway. Dad, however, isn't convinced. He studies me again, letting his gaze linger. "You look like you could do with a good feed, Sarah. If you don't mind me mentioning it."

I do mind, but don't say so. Just nod.

"Right then." Dad goes to put on his jacket.

"I'll go," I say quickly, grabbing mine.

It takes for ever to get served in the chip shop. They're out of cheese and mushroom pies, so I have to wait while they dig out a vegetable pasty and heat it through. By the time I emerge, the sky is wreathed in cloud, the daylight already dwindling.

I take the quick route home round the back of the park, cradling the bag of hot food. It may be August, but the evening wind has a nip in the air that feels autumnal. I should have worn something warmer than my thin summer jacket.

I walk quickly, anxious to get back before the chips congeal into a large soggy lump. Even so, passing the entrance to the park, I pause for a minute to watch a couple of kids mucking around on the swings. A girl and a boy – brother and sister probably. It seems late for them to be out – they can't be more than eleven or twelve – but I'm guessing they live nearby. Most likely in one of the houses that back onto the playground.

The girl, the smaller one, jumps off the swing and shouts something at her brother, and both of them burst into laughter. I swallow down a sensation like homesickness and the past comes slamming back.

"Sarah, jump!"

I'm up the tree in the woods near Aunt Helen's house, back when I was nine or ten. I've climbed too high and I'm stuck.

"Jump, Sarah. Jump. I'll catch you."

I look down at Max. He's holding his arms outstretched, his face tipped up towards me. He still had freckles then, spattered across his nose and cheeks, and thick dark hair he hated having cut.

"Go on," he says.

So I jump. And land right on top of him, his body cushioning my fall. And both of us are laughing, half-winded, but laughing so hard it's almost like crying.

The memory makes me gasp. A pain in my chest like being crushed. I thought he'd always be there, my older brother, to break my fall.

But now Max has gone. And suddenly it's as raw and unbelievable as the first moment I heard it.

He's gone. And he's left me alone.

I clutch the food to my chest, trying to breathe. You'll get over it, everyone says. You won't feel this bad for ever. Time heals everything.

But I'm beginning to wonder. Wonder whether something like this can leave things broken beyond repair.

I stand there, motionless, until my head stops spinning, then set off up Colfox Avenue. The place seems oddly deserted. There are no cars around, except for those parked along the kerb, and no one else out walking. I'm halfway down the road when I feel a chill down the back of my neck, a kind of icy shiver. I spin round, scanning the street behind me.

No one there. But I can't shake the sensation that I'm somehow being watched.

I blink back tears. *Get a grip,* I tell myself fiercely. *Stop it.*

Crossing to the other side of the road, I take the shortcut behind the cinema. But a few metres along the alleyway, I become aware how dark it is, the large firs in the neighbouring gardens blocking most of the remaining light.

"Christ," I mutter, clasping the bag tighter as the panic

begins to rise, fighting the urge to turn again and look behind me.

Walk, I tell myself. But I can't. I give in and spin around. For a second I think I see someone in the shadows, darting out of sight. Fear wells right up into my throat.

I stand there, paralysed, staring into the gloom. But as my eyes adjust to the twilight, I can see there's no one there.

Oh god. What the hell's the matter with me? Why can't I pull myself together? It occurs to me I'm having some kind of breakdown. Maybe it's all got too much and I'm starting to fall apart.

But then I hear the sound of footsteps and I turn round and see him, only a few paces behind me. A man. Tall and dark and eerily familiar.

I let out a small scream and drop the food on the ground as he runs forward and grabs my arm. "Sarah, isn't it? Are you okay?"

I stare at him for a moment, open-mouthed, then burst into tears.

"Oh god, I'm so sorry. I didn't mean to give you such a fright. It's Pete. You know, Max's friend? We met at the…" He lets the words trail away.

I nod my head, struggling to get control of myself. *It's not him,* I repeat to myself. *You're okay. It's not that strange guy.*

"I'm sorry," Pete says again. "I wasn't trying to sneak up on you or anything. I only wanted to say hello…ask how you all were." He bends down and picks up the plastic bag.

Peers inside. A strong smell of grease and vinegar wafts into the air.

I nod again, using the back of my hand to wipe my face, and take a deep breath to steady the thump of my heart. "It's okay," I stutter. "It's not your fault. You gave me a bit of a shock, that's all."

He hands the bag to me. "No damage done – at least not to the food. Do you want me to walk you home?"

I muster a smile and shake my head. "No, really, thanks…I'm fine. Just tired. You know…"

Pete gives me a sympathetic look, and I remember him from the funeral. Sitting at the back with a group from Max's year in college. All of them dressed in black, clearly shocked and bewildered at finding themselves there, in that chapel, staring at a coffin. Like they, too, were struggling to understand how someone they'd known so well could suddenly be gone.

"You sure you're all right, Sarah? You seem kind of shaken up."

"I'm fine really." I grasp the bag. "I'd better get back or these will have to go straight in the bin."

"Okay," Pete says, looking dubious, but I'm already heading down the alleyway as fast as I can.

"Take care," I hear him call after me, but this time I don't turn round.

9

monday 15th august

Coming out of the supermarket, I spot a figure sitting on the opposite wall, eyes fixed on her phone. My heart gives a little skip of pleasure.

Lizzie!

I walk over. She lifts her gaze and sees me approaching, quickly shoving her mobile into her pocket as she gets up to greet me.

"Hey," I say. "You got my text then?" I hesitate for a moment but can't help myself. I throw my arms round her neck and hug her tight.

Lizzie grins as we pull apart and I can't describe my relief. I didn't hear from her all weekend, was starting to think she was ignoring me. That our argument in her garden was actually a break-up.

"Sorry I didn't call back." She goes a bit pink. "It was crazy at the bakery and Mum was piling me up with stuff to do at home."

I smile, though truthfully I'm not sure why that would stop her texting me at least. And clearly she knows it's a lame excuse.

"C'mon," she says, linking her arm through mine. "Let's get a coffee."

We head towards the local Costa. I'm walking on air, buoyant with the hope that everything might be okay with us. I'll talk to her, I think. Try to get to the bottom of what's been going on.

Because I can't bear the thought that anything should come between us. With Max gone, Dad away and Mum out of action, Lizzie feels like the only person I have left.

Inside the cafe, Lizzie insists on buying one of those huge chocolate pastries for us to share. We sink into a couple of armchairs near the window. I stir my coffee, while she tears off bits of pastry and stuffs them into her mouth.

"I'd have thought you'd have had enough of those at the bakery," I say and Lizzie laughs.

"Nah. I never touch the stuff in there. I've seen what goes in them."

I watch her for another minute or so. There's something restless about her. Edgy even. But she does at least seem genuinely pleased to see me.

"Hey, you going to the results party?" I ask, remembering the invite Abigail posted on Facebook yesterday.

"Not sure." Lizzie wrinkles her nose. "Maybe."

I keep my face blank, so she can't read my frustration. The idea of Lizzie missing a major party would have been unthinkable a few months ago; now it just feels normal.

Normal, but exasperating.

A ding from Lizzie's phone. She digs it out her pocket and checks the screen. Shoves it back again with a hint of disappointment in her expression. As if she'd been waiting for something – and that wasn't it.

"So, how's things at home?" Lizzie takes the remaining half of the Danish and sticks it on my plate, wiping the sugary goo from her fingers with a paper napkin.

I shrug. "Okay, I guess. Dad went off to Scotland yesterday, so it's just me and Mum." I don't tell her how abandoned this makes me feel.

"Scotland?"

"Work. Out on the rigs."

"And your mum? She all right with that?"

My mood spirals at the memory of Dad's departure. Mum putting on a brave face, though I could see how much effort she was making to hide her distress. Dad acting like it was nothing, like he was simply popping out for a carton of milk.

That was until the taxi arrived.

"I could cancel," he said suddenly, as the driver loaded his suitcase into the boot of the car. Dad looked at me, then at the house, though Mum had already retreated to her bedroom.

"Go," I urged, standing on my toes to give him a quick peck on the cheek. "We'll be fine. Just go."

He didn't argue.

"Mum will be all right," I reply, in answer to Lizzie's question. Wishing I believed it myself.

Lizzie fidgets with her napkin, as if searching for something reassuring to say. "Look, Sarah, I just wanted to tell you…I'm sorry. I know I've been a bit moody recently…well, for a while. But I want to say it's not you…I mean, it's got nothing to do with us. I need you to know that."

I stare at her. "So what is it, Lizzie? What's going on?"

She sits back. Chews her bottom lip and glances out the window. "It's nothing. It's just…" She falls silent again.

"Just what?"

Lizzie thinks for a few seconds, then opens her mouth to respond. Tries to force herself to look at me straight but doesn't quite pull it off. "There's some stuff I need to tell you. Things I probably should have told you a while ago actually."

My pleasure at seeing my best friend ebbs away as I sense this is serious. And the way she can't meet my eyes tells me what she's about to say is not going to be anything I'll like.

"I'm not sure how to explain. The thing is…" She falters. "Oh god, this is so difficult."

I lean forward and grasp her hand. "Lizzie, it's me, okay. You can tell me whatever. You know that."

She squeezes my fingers in return. Manages a smile. "I do know that, Sarah. That's why I feel so bad about not talking to you before, but—"

She stops. Her eyes widen and seem to fix on something outside the cafe window.

I swing round to follow her gaze. I don't see anything at first. The usual clumps of shoppers cruising up and down the high street. Near the doorway a mother fiddling with a strap on a buggy while the toddler inside arches its back, face contorted in fury. A group of girls are hanging out by the benches – one pulls a pair of red jeans from a carrier bag and holds them up for inspection.

All pretty normal for a Saturday afternoon.

I look back at Lizzie. She's still staring out the window with an expression on her face I can't read. But I can see it's not good.

"Lizzie, what's up?"

I turn again and examine the street. That's when I spot him. Standing on the corner of Bute Road, leaning against the bit between the camera shop and the Italian restaurant, looking directly towards the cafe. Towards us.

Black hair. The same leather jacket and dark jeans.

"That's him!" I nearly leap to my feet as I turn back to Lizzie. "That's the man I was telling you about! The one who ran away. The one with the map."

Lizzie doesn't look at me. The colour has drained from her face.

"There!" I say quickly. "Over by the camera shop. The guy staring right at us."

Lizzie blinks, then fixes her eyes on me, her expression a mask of forced composure.

"What guy?"

"*Over there!*" I point out the window.

But he's gone. Vanished. Almost as if I imagined him. I scan the length of the street, but there's no sign of him. What on earth…?

I turn back to Lizzie. "For god's sake, you must have seen him. You were looking right at him!"

Lizzie gives a nervous laugh and shakes her head. "I didn't see anyone unusual."

I gaze at her, astonished. "So what were you staring at?"

Her cheeks redden. "Nothing. I just remembered something, that's all."

"What?"

"It doesn't matter. Anyway, I've got to go." Lizzie reaches under the table for her bag.

I take a deep breath, then lean over and grab her arm. "Lizzie, don't leave. You said you were going to tell me something."

Lizzie pauses and looks at me. Sort of. Her eyes keep sliding away from mine. "It's nothing. Sorry."

"What do you mean 'nothing'?" I give her arm a shake. "Why are you running away? Why are you being so… so weird?"

My friend seems immobilized. She sits there, staring down at her empty plate.

"Lizzie, please…this is doing my head in. I…I don't know what to…"

I'm close to crying. Again. I take another deep breath.

"Dad's gone away and Mum is still in pieces and I'm starting to wonder if she's ever going to get better. And now this strange guy I keep seeing all the time…"

I glance outside, afraid he'll be there again, but there's no trace of him. "I'm scared," I say. "I'm so behind on my music and the audition's in a few weeks and…and I feel I can't talk to you any more. It's as if this huge gulf has opened up between us and I've no idea why." The words tumble out and I have to bite them off before I start sobbing in earnest.

Lizzie still doesn't speak, keeping her gaze fixed on the table.

"What's happening, Lizzie?" I can't keep the desperation out of my voice. "You've been so off with me recently. With everyone. *What's the matter?*"

She looks up finally and I see all the pain in her eyes. I can tell she's fighting tears too. She opens her mouth as if about to say something, then glances back out the window.

"I'm sorry, Sarah, I've got to go. There's something I have to do and I can't put it off any longer."

She gets up, pulling on the cardigan she left draped across the back of the chair.

"I'll come with you then…" I jump up and grab my bag.

"No need," she says abruptly, already making for the door. She turns before letting it close, her face stricken with something I can't even begin to fathom.

"I'll call you." She wavers for a moment. "I'm sorry."

I reach for my jacket, determined to follow. Lizzie can't just leave like this. What the hell is going on? But at that second my phone rings. I pull it out my pocket and glance at the screen.

Mum.

I hesitate, almost let it go to voicemail. Then relent and take the call. Her voice is hysterical. Her words punctuated by huge staccato sobs.

"Oh god…Sarah…come home quickly. It's ruined. All of it… Everything."

10

monday 15th august

By the time I arrive the police are already there, a yellow-and-blue chequered car parked right outside our house. One of our neighbours hovering by his window, hardly bothering to hide his curiosity.

I almost sprint inside, expecting to find Mum in pieces. But she's sitting on the sofa in the living room talking to a policewoman with short red hair, looking calmer than she sounded on the phone. Stunned, rather than in the first grip of panic.

It's my turn to freak out. My mouth drops as I survey the devastation. Nothing is where it was when I left the house this morning. Every single drawer and cupboard has been pulled open, the contents scattered everywhere. The shelves are empty, their books and ornaments forming a tide of debris on the floor. The furniture dragged away from the walls and the TV pitched off its stand, lying face down on the carpet, a tangle of cables trailing from its back.

I retreat to the kitchen. A sea of food and utensils and bits of crockery greets me at the door. At least half the bowls and plates are smashed, swept out of the cupboards onto the tiled floor. Tea towels are strewn around the room like rags, and there's a large puddle of milk by the gaping door of the fridge.

Nothing has been spared, it seems. Even the toaster is lying on the kitchen floor, an ugly dent in its stainless steel side.

Dazed, I go upstairs, barely registering Mum's voice calling me from the living room. Step over the towels littering the hallway, swept out from the airing cupboard. Glance in the bathroom. The sink is full of plastic bottles and packets of pills, the door of the wall cabinet left open.

My bedroom. A groan escapes me as I walk in. All my books, my sheet music, my collection of old classical CDs, clothes, college folders, everything massed in a heap across my rug. It looks like the news footage from the aftermath of some kind of natural disaster. A tornado maybe, or an earthquake.

"Sarah?" Mum calls again. I ignore her, trying to take in the ruins of my room.

Who did this? And why? Why make such a mess?

I survey the debris on my carpet. Bend down to retrieve the things at my feet, then pause – I guess I shouldn't touch anything until the police say it's okay. But in the middle, partially hidden by the book on vocal training Mrs Perry lent me, I spot my necklace – the silver one with the little amethyst Mum and Dad gave me for my sixteenth birthday.

I can't stop myself. I step forwards and pick it up, praying the chain hasn't broken. It hasn't. Without thinking I undo the tiny clasp and fix it round my neck, a talisman against the surrounding chaos. I'm keeping it safe, I decide – or maybe it's the other way round.

I glance about for anything else that needs rescuing and my eyes fall on a small granite pebble, streaked through with rose-coloured quartz. Odd. What's that doing here? It was my brother's – he always kept it on his desk.

I bend down again to retrieve it, running my finger over its rough surface, and for a second I'm back there, on the island in the lake by our summer house. Max teasing me, pulling faces and sniping till I lost my temper and grabbed this stone and lobbed it at him.

It hit my brother square on the forehead, immediately drawing a small bead of blood. I can still remember the shock on his face, more pronounced than the pain. Then the smile that broke out over his features.

"Didn't think you had it in you," he said.

I often wondered why he kept it. As a trophy, perhaps, or a reminder to both of us not to let things go that far again? Or simply a memento of the place he loved so much.

But what's it doing in here?

"Sarah?" Mum's voice is more insistent. I leave the stone on my empty bookcase and head downstairs, glancing into the other bedrooms as I go. I've never seen such a mess, particularly in Max's room. The sight is so overwhelming that I feel numb. Almost anaesthetized.

How will Mum deal with this? All his stuff, everything she had left of him, ransacked and trashed?

By the front door, I pass a man brushing powder onto the frame, leaving great stains of silvery-grey, like blotches of algae. For a moment I can't think what he's doing, then realize he's dusting for fingerprints.

Where are we even going to start with this? I wonder as I go back to the living room. I gaze at Mum as if she might have an answer. She's pale, her face pinched and haggard, the police officer holding her hand. It's all so like when Max died: the police coming to the house, Mum sitting there, shaking, looking as if her world had caved in.

"What h-happened?" I gasp. "I mean, when…?"

Mum shakes her head. "I don't know. I was only out for an hour or so, at the doctor, then the chemist."

"Sarah, isn't it?" the police officer says with a professional smile. "My name's PC Annie Wilson. Why don't you sit down?"

I sink into the armchair opposite. The cushion is wonky, as if someone replaced it in a hurry. I glance round the room again. I can't take my eyes off the wreckage.

How will we ever clear this up? I wonder for a second time. It seems impossible somehow, pointless, as if we'd be better off simply walking out the house and never coming back.

"Could I check what time you left this morning?"

I look up. The police officer is speaking to me. I give her all the details she asks for, examining her face for clues, as if she might know something we don't. But her expression gives nothing away, even when it's obvious that my answers aren't providing anything useful.

"How did they get in?" I ask when she's finished with her questions.

She nods towards the back of the house. "Forced open a window. They'd have been in within seconds."

They must have climbed over the wall where it borders onto the alleyway, I think, shivering as I picture them creeping across the garden.

PC Wilson leans down and takes something out of the case at her feet. An A4 envelope. She pulls out several sheets of white paper and a couple of black ones. "Do you mind if I take your prints now? It'll save you a trip into the station."

I must look a bit taken aback, because she tacks on a reassuring smile. "It's only so we can eliminate yours from any we find."

"What about Dad?" I say. "I mean, he's away."

"Don't worry. We'll get his prints when he gets back, or the Scottish police could send them over."

I go first. PC Wilson writes my name at the top of a form with a series of boxes on it, then lays it beside the black sheet on the coffee table. She grips my fingers and presses each firmly, first onto the black paper, then onto the white. Little smudgy whorls appear in the boxes. I stare at them, fascinated despite the shock of it all.

My own unique pattern.

While Mum does hers, I examine the dark stains on my fingertips. Will they wash off or will we walk round like this for weeks? I imagine people wondering what we've done, not knowing we're actually the victims.

But PC Wilson pulls out a packet of wipes from her case and hands one to each of us. The black marks rapidly disappear.

As she puts everything away, PC Wilson glances around. "This is pretty awful. I haven't seen a burglary this messy in a long time."

Too right, I think, suppressing the urge to say it out loud. Our lives are shaping up to be quite a disaster.

"We'll be interviewing the neighbours," she adds, writing something in her notebook before tucking it back into the pocket of her jacket. "The good thing is we have a fairly narrow time frame for the break-in, so there's a chance we may turn up a useful witness."

"But why?" I ask, bewildered. "Why us? It's not like we've got anything particularly valuable."

She shrugs. "I can't answer that, Sarah, I'm afraid. I suppose something must have caught their eye. Have you noticed anything obvious missing?"

"My laptop," I say, suddenly realizing it wasn't on my desk. Or in the pile on the floor. I bite my lip in anguish. It was nearly brand new.

She reaches into her case and pulls out a form, passing it to Mum. "If you could both go around later, after we've taken all the photographs, and write a list of everything you notice that's gone. You'll need it anyway for your insurance company."

Mum's hand trembles as she takes it.

"I'm sorry. I know this must be a terrible shock. And coming so soon after…" PC Wilson lets her sentence trail off as Mum's face threatens to crumple, then looks across at me. "Have you got anywhere else you could stay tonight? Maybe for a few days while you get this cleared up."

I think for a second. Aunt Helen. We could go there. But she lives an hour away in Guildford and Mum's clearly in no fit state to drive.

"Shall I call Aunt Helen? Ask her to come and pick us up?"

Mum doesn't respond. Just keeps her head in her hands.

PC Wilson nods at me. "Perhaps that would be best." She pats Mum on the shoulder and gets to her feet. "We'll send over the local Victim Support person. He's very good. He'll give you our leaflet on property security. Window locks, maybe an alarm…that sort of thing."

I thank her, though honestly it seems a bit late for that.

"Do you mind if I have another look around?" she asks. "I need to make a few more notes."

I nod and she retreats into the kitchen. I sit beside Mum and give her a cuddle. I don't say anything. I'm too shaken up and, anyway, what's there to say?

I close my eyes for a few seconds, trying to quell the wobbly feeling inside. But I keep picturing whoever was in here, going through our house, destroying everything.

Why did they have to make such a bloody mess?

Then it hits me. I can't believe I didn't think of it before. Oh Jesus…

I leap up and find PC Wilson in the kitchen.

"How did they know?" I try to work through the swirl of thoughts in my head. "That we were both out, I mean."

She gives me an appraising look. "Blind luck, possibly. Or they may have knocked on the door to check first. But given that your mum says she doesn't go out much, my guess would be that someone was watching the house."

I recall the shadow under the street light and take a deep breath. "I might know who did this."

Her head jerks towards me. "Really?"

"Um…the thing is, I think someone has been following me."

"Following you?" Her gaze is sharp. "Are you sure?"

"I don't know… Maybe." I feel suddenly foolish, imagining what Lizzie would say if she could hear me. I shove my doubts aside. "I mean, I keep seeing him. This man. He ran away when he saw me and…"

Then I remember the map.

"Hang on a minute."

I run upstairs to my bedroom, but freeze in the doorway. Where did I put it? I try to remember. I'm pretty sure I took it out my bag, and put it in the drawer of my bedside table.

I glance over towards my bed. The drawer has been pulled right out and is lying on the floor with everything scattered around it. I pick my way across the room, trying not to step on anything, and crouch down. Sift through the contents – tissues, pens, a lip salve, a couple of old sweets. My iPod. I stare at it for a few seconds, amazed it's still here, then carry on searching.

Where is it? It has to be here somewhere.

I check through it all again, but there's no sign of the fold of paper. I rummage through the heap on the rug, then scan the surfaces of my desk and chest of drawers.

Nothing.

I stand up, my heart beginning to race. I remember where I put it now. Tucked in the notebook I keep for singing, homework and other stuff. Things I need to keep track of. Things I need to do.

Where's my notebook? I recall seeing it on my bedside table just last night. I search all around the floor and under the bed, but there's no trace of it.

What the hell? Why on earth would anyone take my old notebook?

A lump forms in my throat, and suddenly I feel dizzy and queasy, like I've drunk something too fast and it's gone to my head.

I'm scared, I realize. For the first time I feel truly out of my depth.

thursday 18th August

Where ARE you?

I press Send, adding it to the half-dozen texts I've already sent Lizzie over the last two days.

Not a single reply. Not even to the one telling her about the burglary.

Looking up, I see Amanda Godfrey walking up the drive with a bunch of her friends, their faces all fluttery and apprehensive. I watch them disappear into the college building, then check the time.

Nearly ten past eleven. I've been here over an hour and no sign of Lizzie.

Maybe she's lost her phone or it's broken or something? But then, I've left her several messages on Facebook – hard to believe she hasn't even checked there. Lizzie's a complete social media addict; she has hundreds of online friends and usually updates her status several times a day.

I cover my eyes and squint into the sunshine. Finally spot someone who looks like Lizzie heading towards me. *At last,* I think, with a flush of relief mixed with annoyance.

But as the girl emerges from the shadow of the trees

lining the drive, I realize my mistake. It's Tanya, not Lizzie. I forgot they bought the exact same purple summer dress, when it was on sale in that shop at the end of the high street.

"Hey, Sarah," Tanya says, as she approaches. "You got your results already?"

I shake my head.

"Coming in to get them then?" She smiles.

"I'm waiting for Lizzie. God knows where she is."

Tanya frowns. "Yeah, what's up with her? I texted her the other day about Abby's party and she ignored it."

"I've got no idea," I sigh.

"You're going though, right? To the party?"

I nod, though if Lizzie's not going I can't say I'm keen. I've enough on my plate with work and singing without a late night and a hangover into the bargain.

"Okay, well, I'll see you Saturday. Good luck!" Tanya gives me a little wave as she disappears into the building. I check the time again. Christ, the office shuts in half an hour – at this rate, we're going to miss it.

Then it occurs to me that maybe Lizzie isn't coming at all. But we always planned to collect our results together. And surely she won't wait for them to arrive in the post? Lizzie needs pretty decent grades this year if she wants to study journalism at uni – she must be dying to know what she's got.

I feel my irritation grow. Not only for being left in the lurch like this, but there's all the other stuff I need to discuss with Lizzie. The burglary. And the map. Because if the two are connected – and I'm increasingly convinced they are – she should be as worried as I am. After all, it showed her house as well as mine.

Something about her lack of curiosity over the map doesn't add up; it's as if she doesn't even want to consider what it means. And that man, I think, remembering the incident in the cafe. I'm *sure* Lizzie saw him – the guy that burgled us – although she refused to admit it. And I want to know why.

Five more minutes, I decide, glancing at my phone, then at the door leading into college. I'll give her five more minutes and then I'm going in.

Inside, I join the small queue for the secretary's office, my stomach pulsating with nerves. Mrs Ogden sticks her head out the hatch and asks for the name of the guy in front of me, then disappears to retrieve his envelope.

I watch a group of girls from my year open their results together, four pairs of eyes scrolling down their letters. A couple of faces break out into wide smiles. Jane Thomas gives a whoop of delight, but her friend Frances stares hard at the piece of paper in her hand, her face pale and withdrawn.

The guy in front moves aside. I glance along the corridor one last time for Lizzie – still nowhere to be seen – then give my name to Mrs Ogden.

"Good luck," she says, handing me my envelope.

I resist the urge to open it immediately. Go outside and sit on the bank by the sports pitch and study my name printed on the front in neat capitals. Drag some air into my lungs and slip my finger under the flap and slide it free.

My eyes jump to the capital letters in bold print. B in music, a D in drama, a D in English and an E in citizenship.

Oh god. I feel my stomach drop into the ground and have to bite my cheek to take the edge off my disappointment.

I should have got an A in music at least.

Shit. I thought the exams went all right, despite what happened with Max. I thought I'd held it together enough to get reasonable grades. Not great, but okay.

But then I've been sleepwalking through my life for weeks now. What do I know about okay any more?

"Bad news?"

I glance up to see Pansy Levinson hovering a few metres away.

"Could have been better." I shrug. "You?"

She looks a bit embarrassed, like she doesn't want to rub it in. "Four As," she says, her voice sheepish.

"That's great." I force myself to look pleased. Pansy is nice as well as clever and I don't want to make her feel bad.

"Anyway, you don't have to worry," she adds quickly. "You're going to study music, right?"

"Fingers crossed." My fake composure wavers as I quell

another flush of anxiety. I've barely done any practice in the two days since the burglary. It's taken me and Mum and Aunt Helen all that time to clean up.

"I'd better go." Pansy tucks her results into her bag. "My parents will be on tenterhooks."

"You could ring them."

"Nah," she says, finally letting her mouth widen into a broad smile. "I want to see the look on their faces."

When I get home Mum is kneeling by the bookshelves in the lounge, a pile of photo albums laid out in front of her. She's looking at the pictures taken at the summer house that she and Aunt Helen inherited from our Swedish grandmother. I catch a glimpse of Max around age seven, standing on the wooden porch, smiling and wrinkling his nose up at the camera. In one hand, a fishing net on a stick – the kind kids use; in the other, a glass jar full of water, in which you can just see the dark shadow of a tiny fish.

Mum climbs to her feet, closing the album. The corners are a bit bashed from where it was thrown on the floor, but the pictures inside seem okay. Thank god. I can't bear to imagine what she'd be like if we'd lost those.

"I'm going to get them digitalized." Mum picks up the stack of albums and puts them back on the shelf. "Helen's offered to do it. Uncle Derek's bought a scanner and she says it won't even take her that long."

"Good idea," I say. "Then they'll be safe."

Which is more than can be said for the rest of our stuff. Loads got broken, especially in the kitchen. We've had to go and buy new cups and plates, bowls and everything. Even a new kettle.

When Dad called from the rig he said we'll get it back on the insurance, so it's not about the money. What hurts are the things we can't replace. Like the vase Max and I got Mum on her fortieth. And that lovely old clock Dad's grandfather left him, the one with the little pillars and glass-covered dial that sat on the mantelpiece.

Strangely, Mum, despite my worst fears, seems to be taking it all surprisingly well – even the devastation in Max's room. When Dad rang and said he'd come straight home, she insisted he stay put. Told him we were handling it.

On the coffee table I spot the list we're making for the insurance company. "Have you thought of anything else?"

She shakes her head. "I've been racking my brains. But no, nothing."

That's what's weird, I think, reading through the items on the claims form. Most are for things that were smashed or damaged. Beyond that there wasn't a great deal missing. Some cash Mum kept in a pot in the kitchen – only sixty quid or so. My laptop, and Max's – the one he left behind in his room.

PC Wilson says that whoever broke in knew he didn't have much time, or wasn't able to carry anything large. He was probably just looking for money and valuables.

But he didn't take my iPod, which was practically new. Or Gran's gold wedding ring, or the little diamond necklace Dad got Mum for their twentieth anniversary. It was all there, scattered on their bedroom floor around her discarded jewellery box.

It doesn't add up. Why would he leave those, yet steal my crummy old notebook? Did he know his map was inside?

I flash back to PC Wilson's face when I told her about it and the man who'd been following me. How she tried to act as if it wasn't some mad thing I'd invented. Made notes, like she was taking it seriously.

But without the only piece of evidence I had to back up my story, it all sounded ridiculous. Some mysterious guy stalking a seventeen-year-old girl, dropping cryptic maps on a bus – a map that had suddenly vanished. I could see how easily PC Wilson could put it down to the aftermath of Max's death. Grief. Stress. Pressure.

Being plain bonkers.

"Anyway," Mum smiles, nodding at the envelope in my hand, "how did you do?"

Damn. I was beginning to hope she'd forgotten. I'd told her where I was going, of course, but these days Mum lives in a universe all her own. There's no knowing what she takes in.

I hand over the envelope. She removes the letter and reads it. I can't help watching her face. She keeps her expression steady, apart from the faintest twitch of her lips and a small, barely audible, intake of breath before she speaks.

"Well done, darling."

She steps towards me and gives me a hug, but I'm not fooled. There's nothing to congratulate me for. Especially not compared to Max, who took five A-levels and cruised A-stars in all of them. Not to mention a place to study chemistry at the best university college in London.

And made the whole thing look effortless.

Mum releases me, examines my face. "I can see you're disappointed, sweetheart. But it's not your fault. Considering what…considering what you've been through, darling. What we've all been through." Her voice trails off and she looks down at her feet.

I know what she's referring to. Dad asked the college to inform the examining board about Max's death, but they only boost your marks by five per cent as special consideration. Clearly that hasn't made much difference.

"Actually, it's my fault," Mum continues. "I haven't been able to offer you a great deal of support since…" She can't bring herself to finish.

I'm just thinking how to respond when she lifts her shoulders and takes a deep breath, letting it out with a long sigh before looking right at me.

She reaches for my hand and enfolds it in hers, squeezing it as she speaks again.

"I'm very proud of you, Sarah, and I've every faith in

you. I want you to know that. And I want you to know I couldn't have got through any of…of this without you."

She gives my hand a final squeeze before letting it go.

I lean forward and hug her tight so she can't see my face. "Thanks, Mum." I try to keep my voice steady. But despite all my vocal training, there's a tremor there I can't hide.

"I should be thanking you," she says. "And try not to fret over your results. You've another year yet to bring your grades up. Anyway," she adds, making her voice brighter, "you'll have your place at the Royal Music School. You'll be fine."

I blink a couple of times, wishing I could be so certain. The days are slipping away and I don't feel I'm anywhere near ready. Nor, I'm sure, does Mrs Perry, though she's kind enough not to put it so bluntly.

All I can hope – my only hope – is that there's still enough time left to turn it around.

monday 22nd august

I press the reset button on my iPod and "*Ombra mai fu*" pours out, filling my bedroom with its lovely, lilting melody. I've been practising for over an hour, but I'm still struggling with the opening crescendo, and getting just the right amount of vibrato on the high F at the end.

Not to mention the Italian lyrics.

It doesn't help that all the while I'm singing, I'm listening out for the ringtone on my phone, always alert for a response from Lizzie. Every time I've called over the last few days her mobile clicks straight into voicemail. I've left three now, along with several texts and a couple of messages on Facebook.

I even went over to her house on Saturday, after work, but no one was in. I was so anxious I popped in to Abby's party later that night, just to see if she was there. Abby's large, detached home was heaving. Most of our year were there, it seemed, and half the one above. But there was no sign of Lizzie. I went from room to room, and all round the garden, asking if anyone had seen her.

No one had.

It's left me almost sick with misery. It's been a week since Lizzie ran out on me in the cafe, and I can't even think of another time when we've gone this long without speaking.

What on earth have I done to piss her off like this?

One more run through the Handel and I give up. Go over to the new laptop Mum bought me and check my email account. There's a message from Dad. I click it open and skim through. More apologies for not being able to get home yet. Weather bad out on the rig, etc. Will ring soon.

A PS at the bottom. *Don't sweat your results, love. Just focus on your singing and you'll be absolutely fine.*

I grimace and log on to Facebook. Go to Lizzie's profile and scroll through her homepage. There's a post from Finn Johnson, tagging her in a photo taken at college back in the spring. Another from Alice in her geography set, asking about her exam results. Quite a few from people I don't even know – it's beyond me how Lizzie accumulates so many friends.

Both Tanya and Roo have posted on her timeline demanding to know why she wasn't at the party. Sally Donaldson has even sent a cartoon of a sad-looking kitten, with *Don't be a stranger* written underneath.

But Lizzie hasn't responded to any of them. Which is odd. Lizzie's usually religious about keeping up with stuff like that. She'll happily while away hours on the internet, putting up pictures and updates and commenting on other people's status. The week we were on the school ski trip and there wasn't any Wi-Fi, she practically went into withdrawal.

I stare at her profile pic, the two of us hugging and pulling silly faces, Lizzie sucking in her cheeks and lips, opening her eyes wide so she looks like a duck. We took it on the coach, on that Year Eleven outing to the Eden Project. Not long afterwards Lizzie fell asleep, her head resting on my shoulder, and I didn't have the heart to shift it; by the time we got home I was so stiff I could hardly move.

Usually that picture makes me smile. Today it just makes me feel sort of desolate.

God, I can't stand this any longer. I grab my bag, shouting to Mum that I'm going out. She calls back something I don't catch – I'm already halfway through the door.

I walk briskly to the bakery, sweating in the August heat, wondering with each step what I'll do when I get there. Racking my brain as to what I could possibly have said or done to make Lizzie behave like this. After all, she was fine with me in the cafe, wasn't she? At least at first.

I run through what happened again in my head. She came to meet me, she wanted to say something, obviously something important.

There's some stuff I need to tell you. Things I should have told you some time ago.

And then she looked out the window and…

She saw that man.

It wasn't simply that she noticed some strange guy looking at us. The more I think about it, the more I'm sure she *recognized* him.

I stop and catch my breath, feeling dizzy, and not just from walking so fast. Why did Lizzie say she hadn't seen him? Why deny it? It doesn't make any kind of sense.

Was it something to do with what she was going to tell me? I wonder. Could he somehow be the reason she's ignoring me now?

There's only one way to find out: make her tell me the truth.

By the time I get to the bakery, they're closing up. I cup my hands round my eyes and peer through the glass. No sign of Lizzie. She must be out the back, tidying up.

I check my watch – ten past five. She should be finished soon.

Sitting on the bench just opposite, I tip my head towards the late afternoon sunshine, trying to focus on its warmth rather than the tension around my chest.

I'm nervous, I realize. I'm actually scared of seeing my best friend. Afraid that whatever's going on, there's no way back. That Lizzie and I are history.

And that's something I can't even contemplate. Without her, I'd have sunk without trace, I think, remembering when Max died. As I discovered, grief doesn't bring families together; it drives them apart. Mum disappeared into herself, barely speaking to anyone, while Dad lost himself in the practicalities – identifying the body, talking to the police, arranging the funeral. Even Aunt Helen was preoccupied with looking after Mum.

Only Lizzie was really there for me. When being in my house got too much for either of us to bear, Lizzie grabbed a couple of sleeping bags and suggested we camp out in the garden. We lay on the lawn, gazing up at the stars, and somehow having her there made it possible for me to keep breathing.

Lizzie saved my life when my brother lost his. Losing her now would break my heart, and it's this that keeps me waiting, long after the other shop assistant emerges, pulling her cap from her hair and stuffing it into her coat pocket.

Half an hour later Mrs Cavendish, Lizzie's boss, comes out.

"Excuse me." I approach her as she bends to lock the door to the shop. "Is Lizzie Montgomery there?"

Mrs Cavendish straightens up and turns to look me over. "No, she isn't. Are you a friend of hers?"

I nod. "Sarah Marshall. We're at college together."

Mrs Cavendish eyes me with displeasure. "Yes, I noticed you come in once or twice."

I smile. Her face remains stony.

"Actually we haven't seen Lizzie for over a week. Not a word of explanation. I've rung her mobile several times and she's never even bothered to call me back."

I stare at her. I don't know what to say.

"I've no idea where she is or what she's up to," says Mrs Cavendish, zipping the shop keys into her bag, "but when you find her, you can tell her from me that she's fired."

13

monday 22nd august

I walk round to Lizzie's house rather than take the bus. It's well over a mile, but I barely notice. I'm too busy panicking.

She must be ill, is all I can think. But too ill to ring in sick at work? Too ill to reply to any of my messages?

As I round the corner into Argyle Road, I'm starting to imagine something really bad has happened. Maybe she's lying in some hospital bed somewhere, unconscious.

But then surely I'd have heard? Either through school, or her mum would let me know. Lizzie's mum may be a bit scatty, but she's not that hopeless.

Even so, by the time I ring her doorbell, I'm convinced Lizzie is in intensive care, hooked up to a life support machine, doctors shaking their heads as her mum and Toby stand weeping by her bedside. I can see the slow green *blip-blip-blip* of her heartbeat on the monitor, hear the faint whoosh and swish of the ventilator struggling to keep her alive.

I fidget on the doorstep, dreading what I'm about to discover, yet desperate to get it over with. Nothing happens for nearly a minute after I ring the bell. I stand there, waiting, every nerve in my body jittery with apprehension.

Everyone's out, I think, wondering where. Probably at the hospital, I realize, with a jolt of dread that makes me feel almost faint.

I'm fighting a rising tide of anxiety when finally the door opens. Lizzie's mum, her hair swathed in a towel, wearing a dressing gown and an impatient look that shifts to something else when she sees me.

"Sarah…goodness…what are you doing here?"

I stare at her, puzzled. "Um…how do you mean?"

"I just wasn't expecting you back so soon, that's all."

I stand there, bewildered. What on earth is she talking about?

"Where's Lizzie?" Her mum looks over my shoulder.

"I don't know." I glance behind me as if my friend might somehow be hovering there. "I mean, I came round to see her. Is she okay?"

"So when did…?" Her voice trails off as she sees my expression, her look of confusion shifting into unease. "You mean, she isn't with you?"

"With *me*? Um…no. I haven't seen her since last Monday."

"But Lizzie told me you were both going away together," her mum says, anxiety deepening the lines on her forehead. "To celebrate her eighteenth."

"No…I mean, yes, but only to Brighton. We're planning to go down for the day."

Somehow that's looking more and more unlikely, I think, staring at Lizzie's mum. She's not speaking. Just hovering there, gazing with blank eyes that aren't seeing me at all. I feel increasingly nervous and awkward. And guilty, though I've no clue what I might have done wrong.

Besides blow Lizzie's cover.

"Where's she gone?" I manage to ask. "I mean, what did she say?"

Lizzie's mother adjusts her focus to my face. "She said you were going on holiday together. Camping down in Cornwall. Near St Ives."

"Cornwall?" I feel instantly wretched. Lizzie's gone to *Cornwall*? Why would she do that without even telling me? And who the hell is she with? There's no way she'd go on her own.

"How long is she going for?" I say, almost giddy with anguish.

"I'm not sure…ten days or so. I did ask, but she was rather vague. Said she'd see how it went but she'd be back before college started. I didn't think anything of it at the time. You know, she's a sensible girl and I can trust her to take care of herself. But now…" Her voice drifts away.

"Have you heard from her?"

Lizzie's mum nods. "She's rung twice. Claimed you were both having a great time." Her lips press into a thin, tense line.

"So she's taken her mobile with her?" I ask, a heaviness forming in my heart before I even hear the answer.

Her mum nods again.

"I've been calling her," I say. "But I thought her phone was turned off cos it always goes straight into voicemail."

"She said it's not working properly. That's why she can only call me."

I frown, trying to make sense of all this. "But she told you I was there too?"

The expression on Lizzie's mum's face tightens. "Yes," she says, her voice whispery with worry. She pulls up her shoulders and puts a hand up to her head to tuck in a bit of loose towel. "Right. Oh god. I'll try to get hold of her. Find out what on earth's going on."

"When did she leave? I mean, she didn't turn up the other day to pick up her results. I waited ages."

"Wednesday. She left that morning, said she was meeting you at the station."

"But why go the day before our exam results?" I exclaim. "It doesn't make sense. Why not wait twenty-four hours at least?

"She said she wasn't bothered, Sarah, so they sent them here." Lizzie's mum pulls at the skin over her brow, her expression increasingly anxious. "I told her what she got when she rang – not that she seemed interested. She didn't even ask if they'd arrived."

I haven't the heart to ask how Lizzie did in her exams. Suddenly it doesn't seem important. All that matters now is where she's gone, and why she left in such a hurry.

Because last Wednesday was only two days after we

talked in the cafe, and she didn't say a word about a holiday. Surely she couldn't have arranged it all so fast? And who with? Everyone was at Abby's party on Saturday – at least, everyone I can think of who Lizzie might go camping with.

I swallow, feeling weirdly dislocated, like the world has shifted around me, become somehow less familiar. Why didn't Lizzie tell me she was going? Why leave without a word? *I'm her best friend*, for god's sake.

Or rather, I thought I was.

"Do you think she's all right?" Her mum clutches the door frame, her features pinched with anguish. "I mean, should I call the police?"

I shake my head. "I'm sure she's fine," I say, with more conviction than I feel. "She rang you, after all. You spoke to her, so she must be okay. It's just that I don't understand why she didn't tell me. She never said a word about going away."

I don't add how hurt I am. I guess Lizzie's mum can work that out for herself.

"So you've no idea then who she might be with? Not a fella, or anything?"

I frown. "Lizzie doesn't have a boyfriend."

The instant I say it I start to wonder. The way Lizzie kept checking her phone. Almost like she was expecting someone to call or something. Might that explain why she's been so off recently? Some kind of bad romance?

But why wouldn't she talk to me about it? Confide in me? Why keep it a secret?

"I'm just surprised you don't know anything, that's all." Lizzie's mum gives me a sceptical look and I have to swallow to keep calm. I've always got on well with her, but suddenly it's like she thinks I'm hiding something.

And I suppose I am, in a way. Because instead of speaking up about the cafe, about the map and the man that burgled our house, and whatever connection he might have to Lizzie, I shake my head again. "I don't. Honestly."

It's sort of the truth. I don't know anything, not for certain. Just speculation. Suspicions.

Lizzie's mum sighs heavily, tightening the cord of her dressing gown around her waist. "Okay...well, I'll try to find out what's going on." She gazes at me, her expression softening. "I'll ring you if I have any luck. And you'll tell me too, Sarah, won't you, if you hear something? Let me know she's all right? I mean, I'm aware she's almost an adult now, but..."

Her words trail off.

"I promise," I say. "I promise I'll call you if I hear anything at all."

friday 26th august

The film is rubbish, but I don't care. I don't even mind that I'm here on my own, rather than sitting with Lizzie, taking the piss out of the cheesy dialogue. All I care is that for ninety minutes or so I'm not wondering where she is, or why she's gone off without a word. Not thinking about Max, or dwelling on the break-in.

Or that man. I haven't seen him since the incident in the cafe last week. Which confirms my suspicions about him burgling our house – obviously he's got what he was after and cleared off. Though I still for the life of me can't imagine what he wanted with my notebook. Why not simply remove the map, if that was what he was after?

The cinema is packed and there's a huge exodus as the film ends. I nip into the loos by the exit; by the time I emerge, most of the crowd has gone. And that's when I see him.

Just across in the Tolley Street car park, sitting in one of those big black SUVs. Dark hair. The same leather jacket. Watching the last dregs of people leaving the cinema, scanning each face carefully.

As if he's waiting for someone.

My first instinct is to duck back into the loos and stay there till he's gone. But then I remember our house. All our things, tossed around like so much rubbish. The mess, the devastation. Mum's crumpled, defeated expression. I think of what he did and whatever he's done to make Lizzie so anxious and I'm filled with a sudden rush of fury.

I reach into my pocket and pull out my phone. Edge past the sweet stall towards the exit.

I just need to get close enough.

Placing my finger on the camera icon, I take a deep breath and set out through the double doors. As I walk I raise my hand, pressing the shutter button at the very moment he looks round and sees me.

His face registers first surprise, then alarm. He opens the car door and half climbs out, one foot on the ground before he hesitates, glancing at the people around us.

I march forwards, steadying my phone. He ducks back into the SUV, lowering his head and turning on the ignition.

"Wait!" I call out. "I want to talk to you." I step into the road and take a few more paces towards the car. Determined now to ask him about Lizzie. And the burglary.

But as I close in, he pulls out with a screech of tyres that has everyone turning in his direction. A second later I see he's heading straight for me. A wild look on his face, a kind of fierce desperation.

Oh, Jesus.

It's all I have time to think before he yanks on the steering wheel, pulling the car sharply to the right, missing me by millimetres.

I stare after the SUV as it disappears out of view, feeling light-headed with adrenalin, my heart thumping from shock. A few seconds later, a sharp pain in my chest and I sink into a squat, trying to catch my breath.

Oh god. I can't believe I did that. I can't believe what just happened.

"You okay, love?"

I lift my head to see a man standing beside me. A woman behind him, holding the hand of a toddler.

I nod, mutely.

"Bit of a near miss there, wasn't it? You sure you're all right?" He glances down the street, but there's no sign of the black car.

"Someone you know?" He nods at my phone. He must have seen me taking the picture.

I look at him aghast. Oh god, he probably thinks he's my boyfriend or ex or something. Not the man who broke into my house and trashed it.

"N-no…" I stammer. "He's…" I stop. I can't think what to say.

"C'mon." The little kid pulls on his mother's hand and leans in the direction of the park.

"I'm fine, really." I stand up and force myself to appear more composed. "It's nothing, honestly. I'm okay."

The woman gives me a doubtful smile, letting her child

pull her away. The father starts after them, hesitates. Glances back.

"You should be more careful." He walks off, leaving me wincing from the impact of his words.

They sound almost like an accusation.

friday 26th august

The reception area is tiny, a couple of square metres set off from the front entrance, with half a dozen plastic chairs arranged in the corner. I'm perching on one of them, wondering how much longer I'll be here. The place feels cramped, claustrophobic, and smells faintly of some kind of floor cleaner.

The desk sergeant nods when I glance in his direction. "She won't be long now."

You said that half an hour ago, I think, examining the posters on the wall. One is for a missing teenager, a boy with scruffy blond hair and startling blue eyes, who disappeared a couple of years back from a seaside town I've never heard of. The other has photos and identikits of various people suspected of committing crimes. All of them are men, and all look shifty, like actors playing villains in a film.

But none of them the man I've captured in my picture.

I power up the phone I'm clutching in my hand, check the battery icon on the screen again. There should be enough charge.

I'm almost at the point of giving up on the whole idea when PC Wilson bursts through the door. "I'm sorry," she says breathlessly, offering me a warm smile before ushering me into a small room at the end of the corridor. "I had to go out on a domestic. A bit of trouble over on the estate."

I try to return her smile, but it comes out shaky. Suddenly I'm wondering if this is such a bright idea.

"So." She sits at the far side of the desk, gesturing at the seat opposite. "How are you all?"

"Fine," I say too quickly, lowering myself into the chair and trying to act less nervous than I feel.

"Really? That's good." She leans her elbows on the table and clasps her hands together. "Okay, how can I help?"

"I saw him," I blurt before I can change my mind. "He was outside the cinema."

PC Wilson frowns. "Him?" She opens a file with our surname and address on it and flicks through. I catch sight of a photo of our living room, stuff strewn all over the floor.

I dig my phone out of my pocket and press the icon for the photo gallery.

"That man I was telling you about," I say, handing it to her. "The one with the strange map. The one who burgled our house."

"Who might have burgled your house," PC Wilson corrects. "We don't yet have any proof of that."

"You've no leads then?" I ask, as she adjusts the angle of the screen under the fluorescent light and studies it intently. The shot is a bit blurry, his face turning slightly to the side, and the reflection from the car window obscuring some of his features. But you can still make him out pretty well.

I feel wobbly looking at it. Seeing him makes it all so much more solid, so much more real.

"No leads so far." PC Wilson flicks to the next picture, the one that shows him starting to get out of the car, his face concealed by the frame around the windscreen. "So what happened?"

"He was parked outside the cinema, waiting for someone. Waiting for me, I think."

"You? Are you sure?"

I chew my lip, feeling confused now. "It's just that wherever I go, there he is. And it's as if he's watching me. I mean, whenever he sees me, he makes a run for it. And why else would he be there? It can't all be a coincidence, can it?"

"And you've no idea who he is?"

I shake my head. I don't say he looks familiar because I'm no closer to working out why. Probably it's nothing. Most likely he has one of those faces that everyone thinks they recognize.

PC Wilson presses her lips together before she speaks. "Right. Well tell me exactly what you remember."

I hesitate, unsure whether to reveal that I was about to confront him. "He drove the car right towards me. I thought he was going to kill me."

I shudder at the memory. I feel sick, the numbness of shock wearing off to a kind of dread.

"But he didn't hit you?"

"He swerved at the last minute."

"Do you reckon he intended to hurt you?"

I hesitate. If he did, why swerve? Because there were people around? I force myself back. Picture his expression. More startled, perhaps. Desperate.

"I'm not sure," I admit. "Maybe he was just trying to scare me."

PC Wilson puts my phone down on the table between us. "So at what point did you take those photos?"

"I saw him parked over in Tolley Street. I wanted to get a photo." I leave out the bit about wanting to talk to him. It seems crazy now, that I ever considered it. What the hell was I thinking?

PC Wilson frowns. I know, at least, what she's thinking. That I am very, very stupid.

"I don't suppose you got his number plate?"

"No, I'm sorry, it all happened so quickly." I chew my lip again. "I didn't think…" My words tail off. I could kick myself for being such an idiot.

"Okay…" She closes the file on the burglary and nods at my phone. "Do you mind if I make a copy of that photograph? Then I'll take a statement."

"So you don't recognize him?" I slump back in disappointment. I guess I was expecting something more definite.

PC Wilson gives a regretful shrug. "I'm afraid not."

"But he must be local. I mean, why else would I keep seeing him?"

"I don't know, Sarah. I'm fairly familiar with all the troublemakers round here, and this isn't a face I've seen before. But I'll show it around. Check whether any of my colleagues can identify him." She pauses, looks at me. "You say you keep seeing him. How many times now?"

"Four for definite. Once on the street, once on the bus – when he dropped that map I told you about – then another time outside a cafe a few days later. And this afternoon."

"But he's never tried to approach you?"

"No. Quite the opposite. He runs off, like he doesn't want any contact."

"Can you think of any reason he might be following you?"

I shake my head again. "I assumed it was something to do with the burglary, but that doesn't explain why he was there today." Should I mention Lizzie's reaction when she saw him? That she disappeared soon afterwards?

I decide against it. After all, what could I say? That I think my friend recognized him, and then she went on holiday without telling me, but she's all right because her mum has spoken to her? The police won't be interested in that. Besides, my whole story sounds pretty silly as it is.

There's a moment where neither of us speak, then PC Wilson nods at my phone. "Can I borrow it for a sec?"

I hand it over, and she disappears for several minutes, returning with a printout of the picture. She tucks it in our file, then leans forward and looks at me.

"Listen, Sarah. It's good that we've got this. It may help us catch whoever broke into your house. What you did was very brave, but I do need to ask you to be more cautious in future."

I try to meet her gaze.

"What I mean is, you should leave this to us now. We're doing everything we can."

"Okay."

"So if you see this man again, you just call me, all right?"

I nod. I feel chastised. Stupid. How could I have been so *stupid*?

"Don't do anything. Don't approach him, Sarah. He might be dangerous."

It's almost an echo of that father's words, the one who came to check I was okay.

You should be more careful.

thursday 1st september

"*Vivace, vivace!*"

Mrs Perry waggles her hands backwards and forwards rapidly to emphasize her point. "Come on, Sarah, pick this up a little. You've only got a couple of weeks to go and this simply isn't coming together."

I'm almost afraid to look at her. There's impatience on her face mixed with concern; I'm not sure which makes me feel worse.

She plays the bars up to my entry again. I come in half a beat too late and Mrs Perry stops. Doesn't raise her eyes from the piano music. Simply goes back to the beginning and starts again.

I manage to come in on time and get to the bit where I have to hold on a top G when my voice falters. I stop and clear my throat.

Mrs Perry looks at me. "Again?"

This time I nearly make it through. Until I stumble on the allegro towards the end. Mrs Perry pauses, resting her fingers on the piano keys. I can tell she's trying to hide her exasperation.

"I'm s-sorry…" I stutter, pressing my lips together and blinking back the tears. Hoping she won't notice.

No chance.

She turns round to face me. "Sarah…"

There's so much kindness in her voice, in that one word, that I break down. All at once I'm sobbing so hard I can't breathe, let alone sing. I feel Mrs Perry's arm slide around my shoulder as she guides me to the sofa at the other end of the room. I sink down, covering my face with my hands, trying to pull myself together, my breath coming out in short, faltering gasps, like I'm choking.

Mrs Perry sits beside me, watching. Not speaking, just waiting.

"I'm sorry…" I sniff, as she offers me a tissue.

"Nothing to be sorry for, Sarah. Do you want to tell me what's going on?"

I don't. I really don't. I don't even want to think about it. But it all tumbles out, unravelling into words… How much I miss Max…and Mum. The burglary, Lizzie, seeing that man again outside the cinema. That wild look on his face as he drove towards me.

"I thought he was going to kill me," I tell Mrs Perry. "For that second or so, I really thought he wanted me dead."

It's true. At that moment I thought that was what he was trying to do. Run me down. And even if it wasn't what he intended, he came close. If he was trying to scare me, it worked. I am scared – and bewildered.

What does he want with me? Why not just tell me? Why does he keep running away?

I tell Mrs Perry all of it, and about the visit to the police six days ago. I've heard nothing since. Clearly they've no more clue who he is than I have. I'm losing hope that there's anything they can do to sort this out.

Mrs Perry sits, listening and nodding. She doesn't tell me I'm overreacting or imagining things or getting carried away. She doesn't start talking about Max and grief and all that stuff. She simply listens. And when I finally reach the end, she stands and rests her hand on my shoulder.

"Sarah, I had no idea. You poor thing." She lifts my chin so I'm looking up into her face. I manage a weak smile.

"Have you had lunch?"

I shrug. "A cereal bar." It was as much as I could manage in my rush to get here from the early shift at work.

Mrs Perry grimaces. "Right. Well, let's start there."

I sit at the kitchen table while Mrs Perry heats up some leek and potato soup from her freezer. It comes out in a block from a plastic box, so I'm guessing she made it herself. I can't even remember the last time I had soup that didn't come out of a tin.

I feel a bit awkward. I've never been in this part of the house before. But unlike the rather stark atmosphere of the music room, her kitchen feels cosy and relaxed. The work area is decorated with pale green tiles, the shelves stacked with pastel-coloured teapots and mugs. There's a large corkboard on one wall, covered with scraps of paper and pictures of smiling babies and kids. Her grandchildren, I guess.

Mrs Perry pours the soup from the pan straight into the bowl she's placed in front of me. Steam rises up into my face and despite all my worries, the warm, creamy scent makes me almost hungry. She cuts me a hunk of wholemeal bread from the loaf on the table and passes it to me on a plate. I tear a piece off and dunk it in, then wait for it to cool.

Mrs Perry sits opposite and watches me eat.

"Sarah, I don't know what to advise you about what you've just told me. It all sounds horrendous. I know you've been to the police but I really believe you should talk to your parents."

I gaze back at her. "I can't," I say. "Mum's in too much of a state to cope with it. And Dad's still away, more problems on the rig. If I tell him, he'll want to come home and he's already had so much time off...you know, when my brother... Besides, what can he do that the police can't?"

Mrs Perry pauses before answering. "But you'll speak to him when he gets back?"

I nod.

"I am very concerned about you, Sarah. You're so thin, and terribly pale."

I don't reply. There doesn't seem much point denying it.

"Is there anything I can do to help?"

I consider her question as I nibble the bread. What is there that anyone could do? I've not seen that man again, since the cinema. Maybe that will be the last of it.

As for Lizzie, who can help me with that? Tears rim my eyes again as I think of her present sitting on my desk, the card propped up beside it. Today is Lizzie's birthday and I've not heard a word – from her or her mum. No reply to the text I sent this morning. Nothing to the *Happy Birthday* message I posted on Facebook.

Where is she? I wonder for the thousandth time. Somehow I can't believe she's gone off camping in Cornwall, like she told her mum. There's no mention of it online, no photos, nothing. And I've rung round everyone I can think of to see if they've heard something, but no one seems to have a clue.

At least she must be safe, I remind myself. Her mum would have called me if anything had happened. Anything serious.

I wrench my mind away from my anxiety and down another spoonful of soup, buoyed by its warmth and delicate flavour. I'll see Lizzie in a few days, I think, when the new term starts. I can give her my present then.

And when she's back I'll talk to her, I resolve again. I'll make her tell me what's going on. We'll sort this out once and for all.

Simply coming to this decision makes me feel better. That, and the hot soup spreading a glow through my stomach that makes me feel less weepy. I glance down. I've eaten most of the bowl without even realizing.

"Sarah, I need to ask you this." The seriousness on Mrs Perry's face instantly dispels my more hopeful mood. "Do you think you're really up to the audition this year? You could always put it off until you've finished your A-levels next summer."

Her question blindsides me and fills me with a momentary sense of panic.

She sees my expression. "You've been through something terrible, and it's all so raw. It's going to take time to find your feet again, even leaving aside all this other stuff you've told me. It wouldn't hurt to give yourself a bit more time."

I know what she's saying makes sense, but the idea of waiting another year, of not knowing for so long if I've got a place, got a future, makes me feel sick. I don't think I could bear it.

I look Mrs Perry square in the face. "No," I say firmly. "I want to go ahead. I want this more than anything."

Right now singing is all I have, even if it is a struggle. The only anchor in my life. The one thing stopping me being completely cast adrift.

There's no way I'm letting it go, not even for a heartbeat.

monday 5th september

She isn't here.

I look round the common room again, at all the familiar faces, some tanned from holidays abroad, others pale from a summer spent at home. And not one of them Lizzie's.

I spot Roo over in the corner, still eating her lunch. "Hey," she says, as I walk over. "Where's Lizzie?"

"I was going to ask you that," I say, glancing around again. "You haven't seen her either?" It's possible I missed her earlier. I'd squeezed in some practice this morning and only just made it into college in time for first lesson.

Roo puts down her sandwich and curls up her lip, clearly annoyed. "No bloody sign. I'm pissed off with her for missing the party, actually. Didn't even message or anything to explain."

Across the other side of the common room I spot Tanya. I give her a quick wave and she comes over. "Hi, Sarah," she says, giving me a hug. Roo gets in her question before I do.

"Hey, Tanya, you seen Lizzie yet? She's in your French group, isn't she?"

Tanya sits in one of the free chairs. "She wasn't in the

lesson this morning. I was wondering where she was myself. Maybe she's off sick or something."

Roo turns to me. "You not seen her since she got back from holiday then? You said she'd gone to Cornwall, didn't you?"

"According to her mum."

"She didn't tell you?" Tanya frowns. "What's going on with you two? You fallen out?"

"No," I say too fast. "I've been a bit out of touch, that's all. Been really busy."

Roo gives me a quizzical look and I feel myself redden. I can tell they're not convinced.

"I've got to run," I mumble, turning and walking off before they can grill me any further. Digging in my bag for my phone, I speed-dial Lizzie's number. As usual it clicks straight into voicemail. I don't leave another message, but check the time.

Ten past one. If I get a move on I should be able to make it to her house and get back in time for my next lesson.

Lizzie's mum is leaning over the dishwasher, fiddling with something inside. She glances up and sees me coming along the garden path, so I don't bother with the bell.

The door opens a few seconds later. Lizzie's mum looks the usual mixture of tired and harassed, but there's something else. An awkwardness in her manner, like she's embarrassed.

"Is Lizzie home?" I ask, following her into the living room. "I couldn't find her anywhere at college."

Her mum shakes her head. "She isn't, Sarah, I'm afraid. She's still away."

"So when's she getting back?" I'm flummoxed. I mean, it's been nearly three weeks now. Long enough for any holiday – let alone camping in Cornwall.

Lizzie's mum lets out a heavy sigh. "Actually, Sarah, I'm not sure she is coming back."

"What do you mean?" I stare at her, assuming I must have misheard or misunderstood.

"She rang last night to say she'd got a job in a local hotel and that she isn't coming home. At least not yet." She sees the look on my face. "I'm sorry, Sarah. I was going to ring you but I had to go to work this morning…"

"But that's crazy!" I gasp, my mind faltering. "What about her A-levels?"

Lizzie's mum lets her shoulders slump. She looks defeated. "I've told her that, Sarah. Told her she's throwing it all away, but she doesn't seem to care."

"But what about university? Studying journalism?"

Her mum's face clouds and the frown lines across her forehead look deeper than ever. "Well, I think that's definitely off the agenda now." She watches me and sees I don't understand. "After the grades she got in her exams this year, I mean."

"Were they really that bad?"

Lizzie's mum nods. "Not great, Sarah, to be honest."

I'm speechless. Okay, Lizzie said she thought they hadn't gone well, but she always worries about that kind of stuff and gets good marks anyway. A twinge of guilt, as I remember all the revision time Lizzie gave up to support me over Max.

"Jesus," I manage, half to myself. I hardly know what to say or think or feel or anything. "I can't believe it."

An ache blooms inside me. Lizzie. Oh god. I feel suddenly lost. Abandoned. It's only now I realize how much I was counting on her coming home. On being able to talk to her, to finally get to the bottom of all this.

To get my best friend back.

I sink onto the sofa, leaving her mum standing. I have to. My legs won't keep me up any longer.

"Can't you get hold of her?" I ask, bewildered. "I mean, can't you make her come home? This is crazy."

Lizzie's mum studies me for a moment then sits in the chair opposite, perching on the edge in a way that suggests she doesn't intend to be there long.

She wants me gone, I can see that. I'm making her feel even worse.

"Do you think I haven't tried, Sarah? She doesn't answer her phone or return my calls. When she does ring, she refuses to tell me where she is. I went to the police but they won't do anything – they say she's eighteen now, old enough to make her own decisions. There's nothing they can do."

I gaze at her, my mind reeling through the options.

"I've even got hold of her father," Lizzie's mum adds, beating me to it. "Asked him to go and find her. But we don't know where to start looking. After all, Cornwall's a big place."

"I don't understand." My hands are shaking and I press them between my knees to make them stop. "Why isn't she coming home?"

Her mum sighs and leans forward, her expression anguished. "I don't know, Sarah. I have no idea." She clenches her fists, digging her nails into the palm of her hands. "I haven't a clue what's going on with her. Haven't for some time, to be honest."

I swing my gaze up to hers. "How do you mean?"

Lizzie's mum pauses. Gives me a searching look as if weighing something. "I'm not sure quite how to describe it. She's been so…well…moody, for months now. Just sitting in her room, barely saying a word to me or Toby." She bites her lip and stares out the window behind me.

I study her features. I can see a world of pain there. And worry. And wonder if Lizzie has any idea what she's putting her mum through.

But why? I ask myself again. Lizzie and her mum were great together. More like best mates than mother and daughter, ever since her dad left. I guess they felt it was just the two of them – and Toby, of course.

I even felt a little jealous sometimes, watching them. Like I was somehow the odd one out.

"Who's she with?" I ask. "In Cornwall, I mean. She can't

be there on her own. I asked around in college and no one seems to know who she went with."

Lizzie's mum gazes at me. I can tell she's wondering if I know more than I'm letting on. "I've no idea about that either. She won't tell me. But I get the impression she's got a boyfriend."

A boyfriend? Since when?

I stare down at my feet, feeling as if I've been punched in the guts. Lizzie has a boyfriend and she didn't tell me?

But you knew, I remind myself, flashing back to Lizzie hovering over her phone. *You guessed. It was obvious.*

I should have asked her straight out. Made her tell me.

I look back up at Lizzie's mum. "Are you sure?"

She shrugs. "Only from the way she was talking. Nothing specific. I just get the sense she's with someone."

"Someone she met there?"

"I've no idea, Sarah. I'm sorry. Believe me, I've questioned her over all of this, but she won't tell me."

I examine my hands. They've stopped shaking, but I feel washed out and empty. I can't take all this in. It's like finding out that your dad's a bigamist or your mum had a secret love child. You think you understand someone. You think you know all about them.

And then suddenly you realize you don't know a single damn thing.

I glance at the clock on the mantelpiece and get up. "I have to go. I've got a lesson in fifteen minutes."

Lizzie's mum stands too. She looks at me and hesitates.

She must read the desolation on my face because she walks over and folds her arms around me, hugging me tight before dropping them back to her side.

"I just don't understand," I repeat, trying not to cry. "She never said a thing. Not a word. Honestly."

Lizzie's mum looks at me, her own eyes filled with tears. "Believe me, Sarah, I know *exactly* how you feel."

18

monday 5th september

I can't face going back to college. I get to the bottom of Rydon Road and my chest feels tight and my eyes are stinging with the effort not to cry.

Lizzie's not coming back. I can't believe it. I feel winded. Wretched. Wounded.

How could she leave, without a word? Without even saying goodbye?

I stick my earphones in and put some Bach on to soothe myself. Set off home, the sky gloomy and dark as my mood, walking fast, rhythmically, hoping the exercise will work off my agitation.

I don't see him coming. Or hear him. The first moment of awareness strikes halfway along Argyle Street, an arm thrust tight around my throat, stopping my breath.

I jerk backwards and try to scream, but a hand clamps over my mouth and all that emerges is a muffled sound, while the pressure on my neck increases. An overwhelming, cloying smell fills my nostrils. Thick and suffocating. Like heavy aftershave.

A second later my rucksack is wrenched away and I'm

released with a forceful shove. I pitch forwards, losing my balance, my head glancing against a nearby garden wall, dislodging my earphones.

A pain in my skull. A sharp, stunning pain, and the world falters.

I drop to my hands and knees, fighting to breathe. There's a buzzing noise in my head, a high-pitched whine above the percussive thump of my heartbeat. I grope for something to pull myself up with, hearing a low moan I barely recognize as my own.

All at once I'm yanked to my feet. I try to cry out, but again a hand blocks the sound. Summoning all my strength, I drive my elbow behind me. It meets solid flesh. At the same time I bite down on the flesh covering my mouth.

"Jesus!" a male voice yelps, and the hand withdraws. I feel myself being shaken, then a harsh whisper close to my ear. "Be quiet!"

"Let me g—"

"I said *be quiet*!" He gives me another hard shake.

Taking a deep breath, I twist round fast. My assailant loses his grip and suddenly I'm facing him.

Him.

"HELP!" I shout, as loud as I can, but my voice is rough and hoarse and there's no one around to hear.

He grabs both my arms and restrains me. "Shut up!" he hisses, one eye twitching wildly as he glances up and down the street.

He raises a hand and for a moment I think he's going to hit me, but he just rakes it through his hair, his cool grey eyes staring into mine. Something about the intensity of his gaze stops the scream right in my throat. I've no idea what he's capable of, and I don't want to find out.

I sink onto the low garden wall, crying.

"Did you see him?" the man asks urgently.

I try to drag air into my lungs. I have to run, I think. I have to get away. But I can't move. I'm all out of fight and flight.

"*Did you see him?*" He stoops down and grabs me by the shoulders, bringing his face terrifyingly close to mine.

"Who?" I gasp, trying to pull away.

"The man who attacked you. Did you get a look? Or see where he went?"

I stare at him. I have no idea what to say. I start to shake. The shock of what's happening hitting me in full force.

"What did he take?" he asks, more insistently.

I just blink. This is insane.

"Look, Sarah…"

I flinch at the use of my name. *He knows my name.*

Of course he does. He burgled our house. He stole my notebook. Of course he knows my name.

The man spins round again, checking we're alone before crouching in front of me.

"Why are you…?" A sob chokes out the words. I want to run but I know it's pointless.

He ignores my question. "C'mon, Sarah, concentrate. Did he take anything?"

I carry on staring at him. He grips my arm again, giving it another shake. I cry out in pain. My hand flies up to my head and comes back with blood on my fingers.

My attacker looks aghast. "Oh shit… Are you okay?"

I glare at him, incredulous. He assaults me, knocks me over, and then asks if I'm *okay*?

As if realizing what I'm thinking, he lowers his gaze to mine. "Listen, it wasn't me, all right? I'm not the one you should be afraid of."

He lets go of my arm and reaches his hand to my head. My eyes widen in alarm. I jerk it back with another flash of pain.

"Keep still," he says. "Let me have a look."

I feel his fingers on my scalp, gently parting my hair. I force myself not to shrink back from his touch, figuring my best chance is to humour him. Pretend I'm fooled by this whole charade until I can get away.

He draws back his hand and I see more blood on his fingertips. "You've cut your head." His voice softer now. Concerned.

This is mad. *Crazy.*

"I don't think it's too bad," he adds. "Just a break in the skin. You feel all right?"

I nod.

"You sure?"

I nod again.

He sighs, rubbing his cheek, his face restless with tension. Seeing him close up, I realize he's older than I first thought – mid-twenties at least. I notice a small, thin scar running diagonally across his top lip. Make a mental note to mention it to the police.

"Sarah, please. Listen to me. Did he take anything?"

"Who?"

"The bloke who attacked you."

I swallow. *Play along with him,* repeats a voice in my head. *Wait for your chance.*

"My rucksack."

"What was in it?" He scans the street again, his eyes nervous, catlike.

"Only my college stuff," I mumble. I feel sick, confused, my head ringing from the knock it took. Why bother to ask? He's got it after all. "My music. My purse."

"Nothing else?"

I reach into my pocket. Thankfully I still have my phone. "No."

"You sure?"

"Yes," I snap, unable to take it any longer. "Why? Why are you asking me this? Is it some kind of game? Take my stuff, then interrogate me about it?"

He narrows his eyes. "Sarah, listen. It wasn't me, okay?" He steps back, turning right round to show he's empty-handed. "Where is it? If I took your stuff, where have I put it?"

I check the ground around us. It's true, I can't see my

rucksack anywhere. But maybe he hid it, while I was dazed.

"It wasn't me. Honestly." He hesitates, as if he's going to say something but changes his mind. "Don't worry. Forget it."

He's dancing round on his feet now, clearly anxious to get away.

"Who are you?" I blurt. "Why are you still following me?"

"Still?" There's a note of surprise in his voice. As if he doesn't understand. I notice he doesn't deny the stalking.

"Haven't you done enough damage?" I say, my voice fiercer now.

He looks at me hard, and suddenly I'm more afraid than ever. I swallow down a swell of fear, remembering PC Wilson's words.

Don't approach him… He might be dangerous.

He regards me for a minute. Then reaches into his pocket, and draws something out. I instinctively recoil, imagining a knife or some other weapon.

He holds his hand towards me. In it is a ten-pound note.

"For the bus," he adds.

I look at him dumbly.

"You just lost your purse, remember?" He shoves the money into my palm. I take it, my hand visibly trembling.

He glances down the road again. "I've gotta go." His feet still doing that little dance. "You sure you're all right?"

I nod again.

"Go straight home, Sarah," he says. "And stay there, okay? It's safer."

An instant later he's gone.

monday 5th september

No sign of Mum when I get home. I take a mug of tea down to the garden shed, clear the picnic rug off the old wicker chair in the corner, and lower myself into it, ignoring the musty smell and the cobwebs all around me. I'm beyond caring about spiders.

Right now I need to think, and I don't want any interruptions. If Mum gets home soon, it won't occur to her to look for me in here.

I lean my head back against the wooden panelling and close my eyes. Try to run it through from the beginning.

I was on the left side of Argyle Street when it happened, near that big house with the oak tree in the front garden. He must have come up behind me, via the cut-through that leads to the high street. I might have heard him if I hadn't been wearing my earphones.

I shudder, reliving that pressure on my throat. That terrifying moment where I could barely draw breath into my lungs.

My eyes snap open, my heart pounding and my mouth uncomfortably dry. I pick up my tea and cradle it in my hands. It's still too hot to drink, but the heat radiating through the mug is strangely comforting.

Focus on what you can remember, I tell myself, trying to slow my breathing.

The arm around my neck. The shove. Hitting the wall.

I reach up to the lump on the side of my head, now a tight little dome. A slight throbbing pain as I run my fingers over it, making out a sticky crust of dried blood on the hair by my scalp.

I should go to the doctor, I know. Before I go to the police. But for some reason I can't fathom, I can't face explaining to my GP what happened, nor having to make up a convincing lie.

Besides, the man said it was only a skin wound. I don't know why this should reassure me, but it does.

I have to think. Try to sort this out in my mind a bit before I call PC Wilson. I shut my eyes again and his flash before me, the colour of steel. His face, I realize – there was something in his expression. Right from the moment I swung round to look at him. Something that doesn't fit.

He looked worried. No, not worried exactly…concerned.

But what about?

Not about himself, I think, or he would simply have run off. No, he looked concerned about *me*.

That's what doesn't make any kind of sense. If he attacked me, why did he hang around? Why help me up? Why speak to me?

Why offer me that money?

It doesn't add up. You burgle someone's home. You mug them. *Then you give them the bus fare home?*

A sudden cloudburst, rain thumping down on the roof of the shed, like someone throwing pebbles. I glance up at the house. It all looks quiet, undisturbed, the light I left on in the living room visible through the gap in the curtains.

I force my thoughts into focus. *What about my rucksack?* If he was the one that mugged me, where was my bag? Did he have time to hide it? And where?

I scroll back in my mind. All the houses along that bit of Argyle Street have open front gardens, some separated from the pavement by a low wall. I can't think of a single place he could have concealed my rucksack, especially that fast.

Also, I saw him leave, and he definitely didn't have it then. Surely if he'd mugged me, he'd take my bag with him? And why bother asking me what I'd lost if he had it anyway?

The throb in my head steps up a gear, worsening with the effort of thought. I resist the urge to go up to my room and crawl into bed. Remember something about concussion, about not going to sleep.

Besides, I have to figure this out. Now, before I lose any of the details.

Okay, if he wasn't the one who attacked me, then who did? A mugger, I guess, though I hardly look like someone with anything worth stealing.

A plunging feeling as I remember I've lost all my music

and college work. But I can't think about that now. I take a sip of my tea and wince. A soreness is creeping into my throat. A bruised sensation round my neck where it was crushed, and I'm seized by a momentary panic.

What if I can't sing?

Relax, I tell myself, as firmly as I can manage. *You're okay. You'll be fine in a couple of days.* I inhale deeply, trying to try to keep my anxiety from going into free fall, but see those eyes again. Pale and cool as clouds.

Him. He's been watching me – I know that from the map. We were burgled. And now I've been mugged. There has to be a connection, and he's the only one I can think of.

I pick up my phone, intending to dial PC Wilson. Then remember I no longer have her card. It was in the front pocket of my rucksack. Damn. I'll have to go to the station. And soon, because I don't want Mum to know – this would tip her over the edge.

I abandon my mobile and gulp down the rest of my tea. But I can still see his face. The way he looked at me, the way he kept watching the road, as if on the lookout for someone.

And again, the feeling that I've seen him somewhere before. Way before all this began.

Then I think of Lizzie. And realize that if I go to the police, if I get this guy arrested, I'll never get a chance to ask him about her. Because the more I consider it, the more I believe there's a connection – between him and her, and her sudden decision to go off like that.

No, I resolve. I need to talk to him. I know this as suddenly and as forcefully as I know that Lizzie is in some kind of trouble, even though she's pretending to her mum that she's okay. I *have* to make him tell me what he knows.

He might be dangerous. PC Wilson's warning echoes around my mind.

But what about today? The street was deserted. If he really wanted to hurt me, there was nothing and no one to stop him. Instead he checked me over, then gave me the money to get home.

I'm not the one you should be afraid of. Wasn't that what he said?

I am afraid, very afraid. But somehow I believe him. I believe he didn't do it – at least not the mugging.

And there's something else. Something in the way he spoke, something in the way he warned me to stay at home.

I think he knows who did.

20

tuesday 6th september

The house phone rings while I'm getting ready for college the next morning.

"Sarah?"

"Dad." His voice sounds so clear, like he's the other side of the room rather than somewhere in the middle of the North Sea.

"Hey, how are you, darling? Where have you been? I called home a couple of times yesterday and no one answered, and I couldn't get through on your mobile either."

A wrench of guilt. The truth is I've been screening Dad's calls. I'm not even sure why. Part of me wants to tell him everything: the man, the mugging, Lizzie – all of it. After all, I've thought of little else since. But Dad would probably quit his job and jump on the first plane back home, and with Mum not working, that's the last thing this family needs.

And besides, I am far from convinced there's anything Dad could do.

"Sorry, I keep forgetting to charge it," I fib. I feel terrible about it, but it's better than the alternative.

"Where's your mum? Is she okay?"

"Yep. She's off choosing paint with Aunt Helen. They're going to redecorate the kitchen and the living room."

"Really?" says Dad, momentarily lost for more words.

I know what he's thinking: Mum's barely got out of bed the last couple of months, let alone gone off to a DIY store. Weirdly the burglary seems to have had an energizing effect, like it's jogged Mum out of some kind of trance. She even insisted on clearing Max's room by herself, emerging with several carrier bags destined for the charity shop.

The other day I found her cleaning out the kitchen cupboards, the radio on in the background. A few weeks ago she couldn't bear anything but silence.

"Well, that's good," Dad says, recovering himself. "What about you? How's the singing going?"

"Great," I lie again. I've hardly done any practice since my last lesson with Mrs Perry. And now I haven't even got my sheet music.

"When are you coming back?" I ask to change the subject.

A heavy sigh at the end of the line. "I'm still not certain, love. Not for another week, I don't suppose. There's still an issue with a leak on the well head."

"Okay."

"I'm sorry," Dad says. "You know I had no idea I'd be

gone this long. If I had, I'd have made them send someone else, but now I'm here—"

"It doesn't matter," I say. What's the point of making him feel any worse?

"But I called the insurance company, and they're going to pay the money into our account. I've sorted out everything I can this end."

I'm just deciding how to respond when I hear someone calling his name, adding something about a change of shift. Dad says he has to go.

"I'll call again in a couple of days," he adds, hurry in his voice. "Oh, and make sure you charge up your mobile."

I sit on my bed with my new laptop and go into Facebook. Check for messages from Lizzie, or any sign of activity on her timeline. Nothing. I check my emails, just in case. Scroll down the list. Nothing but spam and a newsletter from the local choral society.

No sign of Lizzie's name.

Back in Facebook, I open a new message window and start to type.

Lizzie,
I don't know where you are or what you're doing. I've no idea why you're ignoring all my messages and texts. Your mum tells me you're okay, but I'm still worried, and I have to speak to you — urgently.

Something is going on here, Lizzie. Something to do with that guy I was telling you about.

I desperately need to talk to you. Please.

Sarah xxx

21

tuesday 6th september

He's there when I come out of college. Standing by the Starbucks on the other side of the road.

My heart ups tempo when I see him, and I suppress the urge to turn and run. *He didn't do it,* I remind myself. *He wasn't the one who mugged you, remember?* Anyway, we're surrounded by people – and I need answers.

All the same, better safe than sorry. I grab my phone and punch in 999. Put it back in my pocket with my finger on the dial button.

Ready.

Taking a deep breath, I force myself to approach him, half expecting him to turn on his heels as I close the distance between us. But this time he stands his ground.

"Who are you?" I say, trying to hide the tremble in my voice. My heart beating so loudly it feels it might explode.

Don't approach him… He might be dangerous.

I make myself meet his gaze head on. "Why are you following me? And how do you know my name?"

His left eye twitches. That rapid movement he clearly

can't control. He looks right at me, checking me over, then finally speaks.

"I can explain. Can we go somewhere quiet to talk?" His voice is tense, agitated, and he looks almost as nervous as me. "Anywhere," he adds, reading the apprehension on my face. "You choose."

He lifts his hand to his hair and I automatically take a step backwards, flinching. He bites his lip, inhales.

"Sarah, I'm not going to hurt you, all right?" He closes his eyes briefly then lets out a long sigh. "Yeah, you're right…I was following you. Sort of. More like looking out for you. Keeping an eye on you, making sure you were okay."

I snort. "Looking out for me? You're kidding, aren't you? You nearly killed me outside the cinema!"

His face colours. "Yeah, I'm really sorry about that. I was just trying to get away. I was flustered. I didn't mean to scare you."

I study him. He seems genuinely embarrassed, and my fear fades a little. I relax my finger on the dial button. "And the mugging?" I ask, watching his reaction carefully. Not yet sure I can trust him not to hurt me.

"You still think I was the one that attacked you?" He looks stunned.

I don't reply.

"Christ," he says, taking a step backwards himself. All sorts of emotions seem to be crossing his face. "Listen, I swear—"

"Give me one good reason not to go straight to the police."

He stares at the ground. Doesn't speak for several seconds. "I can't." He raises his eyes to mine. "But you haven't, have you? Because you don't seriously believe I did that. I tried to help you, Sarah." His expression appears almost hurt.

"So why did you keep running away when you saw me? Why bolt like that?"

"I don't know." He shrugs. "I wanted to keep my distance. Didn't want you involved any more than you had to be." He sighs. "God, this is such a mess."

"What is?"

He presses his lips together. Thinks for a minute. Several girls from my year walk past, giving us curious glances. I feel calmer, suddenly, more in control.

"Listen, Sarah, I know how this looks. I can see you haven't got a single reason to trust me. But I'm asking for a chance to explain. For your sake, not mine."

I consider this. In all probability he burgled our house and I should stay as far away from him as possible. On the other hand, it has to be my best hope of getting to the bottom of all this.

"Okay."

He smiles with relief. Then glances around. "Not here, all right? We need to go somewhere less obvious."

I catch the anxiety in his expression, and feel another flash of fear. Who is he afraid will see us? The police?

"The cafe." I point to the little place over by the bus station. Less crowded than Starbucks, but hopefully with enough people around to ensure I'm safe.

The cafe is half full. One man sitting alone near the door, reading the paper as he eats a plate full of bacon and beans and fried eggs. A younger couple with a toddler at the next table. An older couple sitting opposite.

I should be okay.

I order a cup of tea up at the counter. "I'll get you that," he insists as I retrieve my new purse.

"Why?" I say, trying to ignore the overpowering smell of frying meat. "After all, I owe you a tenner."

He crinkles his eyes and I realize he's smiling. "Forget the money." He nods at my mug of tea. "Want a bacon sarnie to go with that?

"I'm vegetarian."

He raises his eyebrows. "Okay. A slice of cake then?" He points to a slab of something dense and dark, probably some kind of brownie.

"No, thanks."

"You sure?" He gives me a quick once-over. "You look like you could do with it."

I wince, wishing he hadn't said that, and sit at a table in the corner. Next to me is a sickly-looking rubber plant, its trunk long and spindly, its leaves curled under at the corners. He picks the seat opposite the window, eyeing the street beyond my shoulder. I stir my tea, trying not to stare at the hair-thin scar near his lip.

"How's your head?" His eyes swivel up to my hair.

"It's fine," I lie. It's as sore as hell, but I'm not about to admit it. Though at least I don't seem to have concussion.

He looks at my bag. "You got a new one."

"Yeah."

"Did you manage to replace all your stuff?"

"Not yet." Not worth telling him how much hassle I'm going to have getting new books from college. Renewing all my sheet music.

"You haven't lost anything?" he asks. "Anything important…private."

"How do you mean?"

"Nothing really." He looks down at the table. "You know, diaries, notebooks. Stuff like that."

Notebooks? I frown at him. "Why are you asking?"

His eyes dart around, looking everywhere except at mine. "No reason. Forget I said it."

"No." I say it loud enough that the couple sitting opposite glance over. "I won't forget it. I want you to tell me who you are. And what the hell is going on. You want me to believe you didn't mug me? Well, explain!" I'm surprised by the confidence in my voice. I sound so determined.

I *am* determined, I realize. I've had enough of being left in the dark.

"Shhh…" he hisses. "For god's sake, keep it down." His

eyes flit around the cafe, taking in the other customers. The older couple turn back to their food.

He chews the side of his cheek and stares out of the window, eyes darting the length of the street. Then pulls out a cigarette packet and lays it on the table, fidgeting with it. The cafe owner looks over disapprovingly, inclining his head towards the *No Smoking* sign.

"Who are you?" I repeat.

He flips the pack from one side to the other. Over and over. "It doesn't matter."

"I found your map," I say. "You dropped it. You were watching our house, weren't you?"

He fixes me with those grey eyes, but doesn't answer.

"Checking the place out, were you?"

"I told you—"

"So was it worth it?" I butt in.

He looks at me questioningly. "Worth it?"

"Stealing our stuff. Wrecking our home."

"What do you mean? I've no idea what you're talking about."

"Burgling us." I gauge his reaction carefully as I say it.

His eyes widen. "You were burgled? Shit. When?"

I examine his face. If he's acting surprised, I have to admit he's making a fair job of it.

"A few weeks ago."

"Jesus, Sarah…" He grips the cigarette packet. "This isn't good."

I frown at the use of my name again when I have no idea

of his. "Are you saying you didn't do that either?"

His head jerks up. "Of course I didn't!"

I keep my eyes level with his. They don't look away. They don't twitch or move. Again that weird certainty he's telling the truth.

"What did they take?" he asks after a pause.

I pick up my cup of tea, willing my hand not to tremble. "Not much. Some money. A couple of laptops." *And my notebook with your map,* I think, but say nothing.

"Not jewellery, DVDs, stuff like that?"

I shake my head.

"Shit," he mutters under his breath.

I narrow my eyes. "So you know who did it?"

"Who did what?"

"If it wasn't you who broke into our house, stole our stuff, who did?"

Again he doesn't answer. And I can't work out if that's worse than an outright lie.

"You do know, don't you? Why else would you ask me about stolen notebooks?"

Get out of here, a voice says in my head. You're sitting having a cup of tea with a criminal. Or at least someone who hangs out with criminals.

You should be more careful.

He fiddles with his cigarettes, gazing outside over my shoulder.

"We need to get you away." He says it suddenly, without looking at me.

I stare at him, astounded. "Get away? Where? *Why?*"

"Anywhere," he adds, keeping his voice so low I can barely hear him. "Abroad. Out of the country, out of the way. Just not here."

I actually snort with laughter, though there's nothing funny about any of this. "You're joking, aren't you? Why would you even suggest that?"

He sweeps his hand across his cheek, as if trying to contain his own frustration. "Look, Sarah, you have to clear off. I can't protect you here. It's not safe."

"Protect me? What from? This is insane. What the hell are you talking about?"

The blood is starting to pound in my ears and I'm aware I'm speaking too loudly. I see him wince before he leans in.

"You just have to trust me."

"*Trust you?*" I explode, not caring who might hear. "I don't even know who you are, for Christ's sake. You've been stalking me for weeks, you turn up everywhere I go, scaring the shit out of me, and now you expect me to trust you?"

"Sarah, please, listen to me…"

I wrench my arm away. "I *am* listening, whatever your name is, but you're not telling me anything, are you?"

"Jack."

"What?"

"My name is Jack." His voice is nearly a whisper. He turns and stares down the couple at the next table, now openly observing all of this. Without a word, they get up and leave.

"Jack what?"

"Jesus, will you *please* lower your voice?" he mutters, furrowing his forehead. "Jack Reynolds. My full name is Jack Reynolds."

Rings no bells.

"Look, Sarah, you're going to have to take my word for—"

I shake my head again. "Not till you tell me what's going on. I'm not going to do anything you want until you explain what this is all about."

Jack sighs again. Lowers his head and shuts his eyes for a second. "Max."

The sound of my brother's name knocks into me so hard I collapse back into my seat. For a moment I can't inhale. "*Max?* How the hell do you know Max?"

"Sarah," he takes a deep breath. "I—"

"You met him?"

Jack hesitates. Nods.

I'm wide-eyed, disbelieving. Why would my brother know someone like Jack?

Then I remember. I finally remember why there was something familiar about him all this time.

Jack was at the funeral.

He was standing right at the back of the crematorium, hovering near the door. I only saw him because I had to go to the loo to get some more tissues for Mum. But I can recall it clearly now, distinctly, as if I'm watching it in a film.

"How did you know him? When?"

"I met him over a year ago."

"Met him where?"

I see the hesitation in his face. His mouth opens as if to speak.

"Tell me," I hiss.

"I…sold him some stuff."

"Sold him some stuff? Like what?" I can't imagine a single thing someone like Jack might have that Max would want. After all, he doesn't exactly look the reading type.

Jack looks at me like I'm five-years-old. "Weed, Sarah. Not much, only now and then. For him and his mate Rob."

Max smoked pot? What the hell? Though why am I shocked? I know it's common enough at university – it's common enough at college, after all – but somehow I imagined my brother was different.

I think back to the Max who went jogging every day. The Max who wouldn't touch fried food or anything containing sugar. My decent, clean-living brother buying pot off a bloke like… I look back up at Jack, my head spinning. "Wait a sec. You're saying you're a *drug dealer*?"

Jack swallows. "Yes. I mean no, not any more. And it was nothing major. Just recreational stuff."

"You expect me to trust you, and you're a *drug dealer*?" I pick up my bag and get up to go. Jack grabs hold of my arm, almost tight enough to make me wince. I wrench it away. Out the corner of my eye I see the cafe owner watching us carefully.

"Sit down, please. Just hear me out."

I do as he says. In truth I can't leave. Not with so many questions left unanswered.

"I need to ask you, Sarah. Did your brother ever give you something? Ask you to look after it for him?"

I frown. "Like what?"

Jack studies my face for a few seconds, then shrugs. "Never mind."

"What's this about?" I'm growing tired of his constant evasion. "Just tell me."

He presses his lips together. Behind me I hear someone come through the door. Jack looks up and checks them out.

"How do you know Lizzie?" I ask suddenly, hoping to catch him off guard.

It works. His head spins back, his expression telling me he knows exactly who I mean.

"You were watching us in the cafe on the high street a couple of weeks ago. You had her house on your little map."

He doesn't respond. Doesn't deny it.

"She's disappeared," I say.

"Disappeared?" Shock on his face now. Dismay. "When?"

"A few weeks ago. She just upped and left. Chucked in college and everything."

Something like relief washes over him. "So she's okay?"

I shrug. "According to her mum." I feel a spasm of anguish, like a stitch from running too hard. I don't tell him Lizzie's not speaking to me.

"Good," he says. "It's better that she's gone."

"*Why?* Why is it better?"

"Because Lizzie clearly knows what's *good* for her, Sarah. And that's what I'm saying to you. I think you should do the same."

"What do you mean?" I blurt, my voice louder again. "What has Lizzie got to do with this? How do you know her?"

Did she meet him at Max's funeral? I wonder. But Jack was only there briefly. I remember looking back, at the end of the service, noticing he'd already left. I'm pretty sure Lizzie never saw him.

"Right." Jack's doing that thing with his hands in his hair again, the agitation coming off him in waves. "Enough with the questions. *Listen* to me. I want you to think about it, okay? Somewhere you might go for a while. Somewhere safe, somewhere it wouldn't occur to anyone to look for you."

"What for?" I ask again, bewildered. "Anyway, I can't just go off like that. I've got college, and an audition in eleven days."

My question is met with more silence.

"Jack, *tell me*," I repeat. "Everything. Or I'm walking right out of here and going straight to the police. Get them to sort all this out."

I'm bluffing but it works. His expression settles into resignation. He leans back, rubbing a hand over his mouth. "I—"

At that second there's a trill from his phone. He fishes it from his pocket, glances at the number. It's a really old model, I notice, a simple keypad with a small, basic screen.

"I've got to go."

My mouth drops open with dismay. "No. You've got to tell me. What has Lizzie got to do with any of this?"

He's on his feet now, fidgeting again. "Look, can I have your number?"

I hesitate, then tell him. I can't see it will make any difference. After all, he knows where I live.

"I'll be in touch," he says. "Think it over, okay? Somewhere you might go."

"Why?" I ask quickly. "Please. Just tell me *why*."

He shakes his head, right before he leaves. "Believe me, Sarah. You're better off not knowing."

tuesday 6th september

As I slip through the front door, I can hear Mum moving around in the kitchen. I try to dart upstairs before she notices I'm back.

Too late.

"You home, darling?"

"Be right down," I shout from the landing. "Just got a few things I have to sort out." I bolt into my bedroom, praying she'll leave it at that; no way I want Mum seeing me in this state.

Lying on my bed, I do the breathing exercises Mrs Perry taught me to prepare for the audition. I'm trembling, the adrenalin rush that hit as I left the cafe still coursing through me. My pulse is racing and I feel faint. I should have had that cake, though I was way too wired to eat.

What should I do? The thought loops round and round my head like a bad song. *What the hell do I do now?*

I run through everything that happened. Everything Jack told me. God, he's a drug dealer. I let this sink in and it makes me so panicky I'm nearly sick. He's a drug dealer, and probably the last person on earth that I should trust.

But what options have I got? I can't get hold of Lizzie and I've no idea where to start looking for her. And it's obvious now she's somehow mixed up in this, in whatever's going on. Jack knows her. He seems to think there's a good reason for her disappearance – though clearly he doesn't want to tell me what that is.

Christ. Not so long ago I believed I knew everything about my best friend. Lizzie and I never had secrets from each other. The minute anything happened to either of us, we'd be on the phone or round the other's house, spilling every detail.

Now I'm wondering how she managed to hide so much.

Downstairs I hear Mum move into the lounge. The sound of the TV turned on to some chat show, little bursts of laughter providing an accompaniment to the low murmur of voices. I wait a few minutes until I'm sure she's engrossed, then go into Max's bedroom, closing the door quietly behind me.

The place looks more abandoned than ever. All Max's things, at least what was left after Mum's charity purge, have been put back, only more neatly. It gives the room a starkness it never had before, as if it has finally let go of him entirely.

Oh Max… His face flashes up in my mind. The way he'd snigger when I said something he thought was stupid. Whenever we argued, he'd get this sneery expression that made me want to punch him. Like I was a complete idiot.

But now? If Max were here now and I told him all this, everything that's been going on, everything I suspected, would he pull that face? Would he laugh and tell me not to be so ridiculous?

I feel a dull stab of pain as something twists inside. Because I wouldn't mind. I wouldn't mind at all. Max could smirk at me for ever if only he were here – and all this was some big, crazy mistake.

I sit on his bed. Wait for the ache to fade, then force myself to go over Jack's reaction to the burglary. His question about what they stole. I mentally rehash the list we made for the police and the insurance company. Just the cash, a couple of laptops. And my notebook.

No jewellery. Nor my new iPod. Surely anyone burgling a place would want those? They're small and valuable, easy to carry, and yet they left them.

Why? I ask myself again.

This time I have an answer. *Because they weren't after our valuables at all.* They weren't robbing us for money, though they helped themselves to the cash that was lying around. No, they were searching for something else, something specific. It's the only explanation that makes sense.

More than that, they were clearly searching for something to do with my brother. I asked Jack what all this was about, and he said Max.

Leave me alone, Sarah.

A sudden surge of anger. No, Max, you got that wrong, I think. You left *me* alone, alone with this mess. You left me to deal with whatever you did to bring this trouble to our doorstep.

I take a deep breath, blinking back the urge to cry, then begin at one end of his desk, picking everything up and checking underneath. I rifle through drawers. Hold books up by their covers and shake out the pages. I work my way through the room methodically, but unlike whoever broke into our house, I cover my tracks, replacing each item exactly as I find it.

I look under his bed and inside the ring binders on the shelves, then start on the stuff in his cupboard. Most of it is rubbish. Old games and piles of exercise books from school – things Mum obviously still hasn't the heart to throw out.

The trouble is that I have absolutely no idea what I'm searching for. What whoever broke in here was after.

Did they find it? Have they taken it already? I'm guessing not. Why else would someone mug me for my rucksack? Because they hadn't got what they wanted when they ransacked our house.

Or maybe Mum threw it out, when she was going through his stuff. Sent it off in one of those charity bags.

I give up. Sit back on the office chair by the desk and spin it slowly, looking around.

What was Max hiding? What could my brother have had that anyone would want so badly?

I think about Jack and I think about Max taking his drugs. Nothing unusual in that, I know. I'm not that naïve.

But I don't believe it's drugs I'm looking for. After all, it's not as if they're so difficult to get hold of.

No, whatever Max had must be much more precious. This bloke Jack knows what it is, but it's clearly something he doesn't want to divulge. I've never met anyone so evasive. The way his eyes dart around, rarely settling on mine. That twitch in his eyelid when he's nervous. Or lying.

Jack won't tell me, I'm pretty sure of that. But I know someone who might.

I punch a text into my phone. Just one line. This time I've a feeling it won't be ignored.

I know about Jack.

I press Send. And wait.

I'm finally drifting into sleep when I hear a short burst of melody from my mobile. I get out of bed and look at the screen. Someone has sent me a message.

Lizzie!

Go on to Facebook.

I log in on my laptop and see a green light by her name. I click on the chat icon. Seconds later a message appears.

Sarah? Are you there?

Yes, I type, my heart beginning to race. I glance at the clock in the bottom corner. Midnight. Jesus.

Sarah... A pause while she replies. *...are you okay? I've been worried sick.*

Funny way of showing it, I think, watching the words unrolling onto the screen.

...I'm sorry, Sarah. I'm so sorry for all of this. Please believe me.

Where are you? I write.

In an internet cafe.

At this time? Surely Cornwall doesn't have places that stay open so late. *Where, exactly, Lizzie?*

There's a pause. Then one word.

Madrid.

SPAIN!!! I type. *I thought you were in Cornwall??*

Another long pause.

Sorry. That's just what I told Mum. So she wouldn't freak out.

So that's why her mobile is always off, I realize, remembering the different dial tone you get when you ring abroad. Lizzie doesn't want anyone to know she's left the country.

Christ, Lizzie, what are you doing in Spain? And why did you go off without telling me? Your mum's in a terrible state. Everything's just awful.

I'm sorry, Lizzie replies. *I'm really, really sorry.*

I wait, then more words spill onto the screen. *Sarah, listen...Jack...what do you mean you know about him?*

I stare at her question, letting the implication sink in. So it's true. Lizzie knows who I'm talking about.

She knows Jack.

I spoke to him today, Lizzie. But he won't tell me what's going on. Who is he? What's this all about? I'm typing so fast my fingers are a blur.

I watch the space under what I've written for Lizzie's reply, but there's nothing for several minutes. As if she's considering what to say.

Or maybe talking to someone, it occurs to me. Her boyfriend.

Lizzie? My fingers fly over the keyboard. *Are you still there?*

A few more seconds, then she replies. *Listen, I've got to go…I'm running out of time. Look, be careful, Sarah, okay. I can't go into it all now, but I will. I promise.*

Into what?

Stay away from Jack. He's bad news, Sarah. We'll talk soon, all right? By phone, no emails.

Why not? I write quickly.

I'll explain next time. Sorry. And please don't tell anyone you've spoken to me, not even Mum.

The words stop for a moment. Then another message appears.

Whatever you do, don't tell Jack.

An instant later, before I have a chance to type anything back, Lizzie signs out.

23

wednesday 7th september

Meet me. The Dog and Rose. 4 p.m.

The text arrives the next day, no name attached. But I don't care. Only one person could have sent it.

I agonize through all my lessons, wondering if I'll go. Lizzie's words hovering at the back of my mind as I try to focus on my work.

Stay away…he's bad news.

But I figure there's nothing much he can do in a pub full of people. So I head there after college and find him standing near the back, playing on a fruit machine. It's a quiet time, only a few people scattered around the other tables. I glance at the barman, but he's oblivious, watching a game of rugby on the large screen above the pool table.

I stand to the side of the fruit machine and wait for Jack to finish. He's wearing a short-sleeved T-shirt and the same dark jeans, so blue they're nearly black. And a relieved expression when he lifts his head and sees me.

"You came." He turns to face me, sticking his fingers into the front pockets of his jeans and hunching his shoulders up.

I nod.

He gazes at me for a few seconds, as if he's not sure I'm real. Clearly he wasn't expecting me to show up.

"Want a drink?" He gestures in the direction of the bar.

I shake my head. "I can't."

Jack raises an eyebrow.

"I'm not eighteen till February."

A twitch of his lips. "Sorry. I forgot."

"So why are we here?" I ask as he grabs a bottle of beer from a nearby table and takes a swig.

"Sure you don't fancy anything else? Coke? Ginger beer? Lemonade?"

I stare at him. Is he taking the piss? "I'm fine," I say. "Tell me what you want."

He nods towards the beer garden. "How about we go outside?"

We sit at one of the wooden benches ranged around the little patio. Beyond is a small, scrubby piece of lawn with a plastic climbing frame. I shiver. It's early September and though the sun is out, there's a damp autumnal feel to the air. I glance around. We're all alone, except for a couple sitting a few tables away, feeding crisps to a chubby chocolate Labrador.

Jack shifts in his seat and fixes his gaze a little to the left of me, his face tense and determined. "I can explain, but you've—"

"Explain now, or I'm leaving."

"Sarah, please…"

"Lizzie. My friend, the one from the cafe."

Jack nods.

"I spoke to her last night. She seems to know you. And she reckons you're bad news."

"What did she say?"

I counter his question with one of my own. "So how do you know her?"

Jack eyes me warily. I can see him calculating what to tell me. "I only met her once. At a party."

"Where?"

"London. It was after some gig. She was there with Rob, and your brother."

A hitch in my breath as his words smack right into me. Lizzie was at a party in *London*? With my brother and his best friend? What the...? How come she never said anything?

"When was this?" I manage to ask.

"Around May sometime."

I think back. The news of Max's death a month later pretty much knocked everything else out my head, but I do recall Lizzie mentioning a party. That's right – it was the night I was soloing in a concert for the local choral society, so I couldn't go.

I'd assumed the party was something to do with college. Not in London.

"She was with Rob, you say? Max's friend?"

Jack nods.

"You mean they were together?"

"Uh-huh."

A molten surge of betrayal erupts inside me. Lizzie's well aware of how I feel about Rob. All that time he and my brother spent together – even sharing a house in their second and third years – and Rob still couldn't be bothered to come to Max's funeral.

Jesus. Lizzie never said a thing. Not a word. I mean, how come she even met him?

Then it clicks. Last summer. Rob came to stay at ours for a few days. Max invited loads of people round while Mum and Dad were on holiday in Italy and I remember Lizzie spending ages talking to him. I assumed she was asking about university, stuff like that.

"So you didn't know about Rob and Lizzie?"

I raise my eyes to find Jack examining my face. Press my lips together, suppressing a sigh. "It seems there's quite a lot my best friend forgot to mention."

"I guess it's hard to know who to trust." Jack's eyes linger on mine.

"Yeah. You could say that."

"Like me, for instance."

I don't say anything, but have to turn my head away.

"Would it help if I told you I'm actually looking out for you here, Sarah?"

I spin back to face him. "It would help if you told me what the hell is going on. Like why you're involved in my life. And why you'd give a damn about me, anyway."

This time it's Jack who shifts his gaze, his hand fidgeting

around his bottle of beer. "Your brother. He got himself in a shitload of trouble before he died. And some of it…a lot of it was my fault. I figure that watching out for you is payback, that's all."

For a moment I feel oddly flat. As if part of me was hoping for a different answer. I pull myself together. "What kind of trouble?"

Jack stays silent, and for minute or so I tune into the sound of a piano concerto playing somewhere nearby, barely audible under the noise of the TV.

"I want to know, Jack. Seriously. I'm going to leave unless you tell me."

He looks up, measuring my resolve. And despite my show of bravado, I hesitate. Because I can see in his face, in its serious, almost severe expression, that there'll be no going back. The old Max will be forever replaced in my mind with another version – and possibly one I don't like.

That picture flashes into my mind, the one in Mum's photo album. Max standing on the porch in Sweden, holding the jar with the minnow. Looking so proud, and so pure. Still untouched by life.

But he's your brother, says a voice in my head. *You have to know the truth. Otherwise you'll spend the rest of your life wondering.*

"Tell me."

Jack scrutinizes me for a full minute or so. His features barely move, but I can see a battle raging inside. The grip of indecision.

Finally he drains his remaining beer and places the bottle in front of him, cradling it between both hands. "Max and Rob, they came up with a way of making a new kind of dove."

"Dove?"

"Ecstasy. You know, E."

I stare at him, eyes widening. I can hardly breathe. I mean, marijuana is one thing, but this sounds way more hardcore.

Jack was right. I'm already regretting asking him anything.

He shrugs at my expression. "You said you wanted to know."

"You can *make* it?" I frown.

"Yeah. Not easily. You've got to have the right gear. The right chemicals and equipment. But it was easier for Max and Rob – they had the facilities, and the know-how."

I recall the chemistry labs at the university. I visited them once, the first time I went to see Max in London. They were housed in a new, purpose-built block, all pristine white walls and bright overhead lighting, and filled with test tubes and flasks and bottles of interesting-looking liquids and compounds.

Dead smart. They were one of the main reasons Max chose to go there. I remember his face as he showed me around – so pleased and excited.

"He – your brother – said they were only mucking about. Trying to cook up a bit for themselves and their mates. Not out to make money or whatever. Anyway, it worked better than they ever imagined."

"How do you mean?" I sit on my hands and clamp my lips together so Jack can't see them quivering.

"Max and Rob were making a batch and they were short of some chemical or other. I've no idea what. I honestly don't know that much about it. I only sold the stuff."

"Their stuff?"

Jack glances at me but ignores my question. "So Max substituted it with another compound, something similar. It seemed to work. He and Rob tried it that weekend, only a small dose."

I still can't get my head around Max doing this. Not just taking drugs, but actually making them. Why would he even do that?

"So what happened?" My jaw so tense now I have to force out the words.

Jack laughs. But not a happy kind of laugh. The kind of laugh that makes me want to grab my bag and run out the pub.

But I have to hear this out.

"Heaven, Sarah. That's what happened. It lasted twice as long as ordinary E, with no comedown, no feeling like crap for a day or so – you simply float back down to normal. Max and Rob, they discovered super-E – by accident."

Jesus. I've never met anyone who's taken ecstasy – at least

not till now. But I'm not stupid. I understand what this means. And how it might lead to the shitload of trouble Jack referred to.

I glance up and catch him assessing me again. And wonder what he thinks of this naïve girl who doesn't know what dove is – or how it makes you feel.

"So where do you come into all this?" I ask.

"Like I told you before, I'd been supplying weed to them for a while and we sort of became friends. He was a good bloke, your brother. Funny, you know, clever in the way he looked at things."

Despite everything I smile. He's right. Max was witty – and amusing. He could always diffuse an argument by making people laugh.

"Anyway, one evening I hung around for a smoke," Jack continues. "And they gave me some of their stuff, to see what I thought."

"And?"

He twirls his beer bottle between his fingers and sighs. "I thought it was a goldmine, Sarah, to tell you the truth. Worth a fortune in the right hands."

"Or rather the wrong ones," I add, watching him grimace in response. He abandons the bottle and pulls out a pack of cigarettes from his pocket.

"So you offered to sell it for them?"

Jack stares at the pack. He can't lift his eyes to mine. "Sort of. But they weren't interested in making money. They were only in it for the ride. I told them it could earn them loads, enough to wipe out their student loans with plenty left over, but they didn't care."

"So what did you do?"

He twists the cigarette pack in his fingers. And it's then that I see that mine aren't the only ones trembling. This is hard for him, I realize, and I wonder why. Shame? Guilt?

"I...um...went to see one of my contacts. Gave them a sample Rob had given me."

"Rob asked you to do that?"

Jack's face begins to flush. His left eye twitches, then he blinks. "Not exactly. I cadged a couple, said I was off to a party and needed a bit of a lift. Only I never took those, just pretended I had. I was hoping that maybe my contacts could find out what was in it."

Oh god. Ice forms in my stomach. I'm not sure where this is going but instinctively sense it's not good. "And did they?"

Jack shakes his head. "No. They couldn't identify anything other than the usual compounds."

"So why didn't you ask Max? Or Rob?"

"You reckon I didn't? I practically begged them to tell me what was in those pills. But Max wasn't stupid, Sarah. He was keeping it to himself, and he made Rob promise to do the same."

"Why?"

"I dunno. He could be weird, your brother. Pretty straight up over stuff. He didn't want loads of people getting into it, he said, didn't need that on his conscience."

I remember how Max used to berate Dad for using weedkiller in the garden, or have a go at Mum for buying food with loads of air miles. Jack's right. He could be very high-minded about things.

"So what has all this got to do with me?" I ask, wishing I'd accepted Jack's offer of a drink. Right now I could do with something alcoholic. I glance indoors at the landlord, still absorbed in the game – it's not as if he would notice.

Jack sighs. Plays with the lid of his cigarettes, flipping it up and down with his thumb.

"Those people I spoke to. They didn't just lab test the drug, they tried it. Not much – there wasn't much – but enough for them to see its potential. I said I'd talk to Max, try to work out some kind of deal. But then…"

He stops, peers down at the ground between the slats of the table.

"Then what?" I can barely keep the impatience from my voice.

"Then it happened."

"*What?*" My throat is dry and raspy and the words come out as a croak. "What happened?" A tight, almost nauseous feeling in my belly.

He looks past me, towards the climbing frame, and some kind of shutter comes down over his face. "Sarah, look, you don't need to know…"

"Just tell me, Jack." His name tastes sour in my mouth, like something that's curdled.

170

His head turns back to me. I hear him suck in his breath. "Okay…that night…when I met your friend Lizzie… We'd all gone to this gig in town, then on to a party at some student house. Max and Rob, Lizzie and Anna."

"Anna?" I cut in. "Who's Anna?"

He frowns at me, surprised. "Your brother's girlfriend."

Max had a *girlfriend*? He never said anything about her. Didn't even mention having met anyone. I cast my mind back to the people he introduced me to that time in London, but can't recall anyone in particular. Certainly not an Anna.

But I must have seen her. She would have been at the funeral.

"Anyway, Max had some of his gear," Jack says. "Gave it to a few of his friends, people he knew. Then…well… Anna…she collapsed."

I feel the blood drain from my face as I sense what's coming. "Collapsed? You mean from taking the drug?"

Jack sighs. "Possibly. Probably. No one was sure. They did all these tests but they couldn't say exactly what had caused it, but…"

"You mean she *died*?"

Jack's hands lift to his hair. I hear a slight catch in his breathing and my stomach starts to hurt before he even says the words. "In the ambulance. On the way to hospital. Heart failure."

Heart failure. My skin chills at the coincidence. Max

died of heart failure too. Though there'd been no mention of any drug.

Jack flashes me a brief, anxious look. "We did everything we could, Sarah. Tried to resuscitate her and all that, but it didn't help. Her heart just stopped and even the paramedics couldn't get it going again."

"Oh Christ…" I bend forward, trying to breathe. "Oh Jesus…that poor girl."

I feel a wrench of dread for Max. Did he love her? How terrible that must have been, seeing her die. No wonder he was so miserable when he came home.

And Lizzie… I'm starting to understand why she's been acting so oddly since then. And why she hasn't been able to say anything. She witnessed a girl's death…at the hands of my brother. Oh Jesus, how could she tell me that? There we were, me and Mum and Dad, racked with grief at Max's death, and all the time Lizzie was nursing this terrible secret.

"It was a bloody mess." Jack leans his elbows on the table and lowers his forehead into the heel of his hands. "The police talked to everyone who was there, but luckily no one pointed the finger at your brother. Not that he cared by then."

Suddenly he looks up and his pale eyes lock on mine. They look hungry, almost wolf-like, as if hunting for something in me. Forgiveness? Absolution?

"He completely freaked out, was practically ready to hand himself in. I told him it wasn't his fault, that he wasn't to know. Told him over and over again. That Anna could have had a weak heart, whatever. It didn't have to be the drug. As it was, they found nothing at the post mortem, so the police assumed it was natural causes and didn't take it any further."

"But Max still thought it was his super-E that was responsible? Even though they found no trace of it in her system?"

"He reckoned maybe you metabolize it really fast or something. Said just because they didn't find any, that didn't mean it wasn't what killed her."

Jack sighs, takes another breath, as if steadying himself to continue. "He was a wreck. It happened right before his final exams too. He sat them, but according to Rob they went badly."

I remember that last week. The evening Mum made lasagne, Max's favourite, and he actually ventured out of his room, though still looking pale and subdued. Remember Dad cracking a joke about how he must have had his heart broken, and Max getting up and walking out without a word.

Just leave me alone, Sarah.

Oh god. I feel a lurch of pain for my brother that radiates right through me, leaving my head reeling and my breath ragged. Jack doesn't speak for a while, only watches me for a moment or two, then looks away.

Giving me a little privacy.

"I still don't understand," I whisper eventually, my voice

somehow lost to me. "I still don't get why you're here."

Jack's jaw tightens and he looks back down at the cigarette packet. He's gripping it so hard the edges are caving under the pressure. When he speaks, his voice is quiet. I strain to catch it over the traffic noise from the nearby road.

"The gang. I went back and told them to forget it. Told them what had happened and that Max and Rob weren't going to make any more. But…let's say they're not the kind of people who take no for an answer."

I look up at him, a heavy feeling forming in my chest. Slowly I am beginning to understand. And at the same time wishing I were anywhere but here, not having to hear any of this.

"They came after Rob and Max. Paid them a visit. And not the sort you'd welcome, Sarah, if you see what I mean."

I think I do. I remember that pressure around my neck – the brute force of it – and have to swallow before I can speak. "Do you know what happened?"

Jack shakes his head again. "But I can guess. These people can be very persuasive."

"So Max told them how to make the drug?"

"I don't think so. Because the next thing, he and Rob both disappeared."

Disappeared.

Finally I get it. Why Max was in Sweden when he died. He'd gone there to get away…to *hide*.

Oh god. I'm nearly choking on my own breath. Did *they* find Max? Did *they* kill my brother and somehow cover it up?

Indeterminate cause. That's what the pathologist said. They knew Max's heart had stopped but they couldn't say why; especially as the farmer who keeps an eye on our cottage didn't find him for a week. We assumed his death was natural, something Max was born with. A defect, ticking away like a time bomb.

Stupid, I think now, looking back. We should have guessed something was up, given how Max behaved when he came home. We just thought he was exhausted from all the stress of his exams.

I close my eyes, imagining the hell my brother went through that week with us. His girlfriend dead, the threat of the police discovering his involvement, the knowledge that this gang weren't going to let it go.

And flunking his final exams too – the university told Dad he hadn't done well, but Max must have known that already. Knew he'd screwed up his degree. His whole future.

I turn to face Jack. "That gang…Max…do you reckon they…?"

Jack gazes back, his pale eyes softer now. "I doubt it. If they'd found him, things would be different. He might still have wound up dead, but they'd have got what they wanted. They wouldn't still be trying to get their hands on that formula."

"So they haven't got it? The method for making this drug?"

Jack turns down the sides of his mouth. "Not yet."

"How can you be so sure?"

Jack stays silent and then I understand. *Not yet.* The implication of his words slowly dawns on me.

The burglary. The man who snatched my bag. Oh Christ…*they're still after it.*

A chill seeps through my limbs as Jack leans across the table and rests his hand on mine. "You understand, don't you, Sarah, how much this is worth to them? How they're going to keep on until they get what they want."

"But how do they know?" I ask, withdrawing my hand. "That there's anything to find? Maybe Max destroyed all trace of it, you know, after that girl…" I can't even bring myself to say it.

Jack leans back in his seat. "He kept notes. On how to make it."

"How can you be sure?"

He sighs. Sweeps his gaze away from mine. "I was round their house once. He popped out, to get a few beers. I had a poke around. Found a notebook with stuff written down; I'm no chemist, but I recognized some of the ingredients. The basic process."

"So?" I shrug. "What makes you think he didn't burn it or something."

Jack looks at me. "Do you believe Max would? Something that big?"

I gaze back at him. He's right. I'm not sure either that Max could have brought himself to get rid of it. It was too big, too important. Perhaps, in the right hands, it might even have led to something good.

"So you told them? The gang?"

His eyes dart away again. "Only in passing. I didn't mean…I never thought…" He inhales. Fiddles with his pack of cigarettes. "You're right. A lot of this is my fault."

I bite my lip, look back at the pub, the scrap of lawn, the houses beyond. Anywhere but at Jack. I don't feel angry exactly. Just exhausted.

And scared.

"Do you get it now, Sarah? Why I'm here? Why I believe it'd be safer if you went away?"

I exhale. Force myself to speak. "You mean like Lizzie? I don't get that. Why would they go after her?"

Jack sits back and shrugs. "They might reckon she knows how to make it. Or more likely they'd use her to bargain with her boyfriend."

Rob. Now I understand why he didn't show up at my brother's funeral. He must have thought they'd killed Max. He must have been scared shitless.

"But I still don't see how they could use Lizzie to get to Rob," I say.

Jack looks at me as if I'm totally clueless. "Threaten to hurt her unless he hands it over. Flush him out. I didn't see much of them together but it looked as if Rob was pretty serious about your friend. I'm guessing he's been trying to get her away for a while."

Hence Spain, I realize. Far enough for them both to be out of harm's way.

I hope.

A worm of pure fear unfurls in my stomach. "Is that why you think I'm in danger? I mean, Max is already dead. What would they gain by hurting me?"

"You're their last resort, Sarah." Jack pinches the bridge of his nose. "If there's any chance Max might have involved you, given you those notes to hide, for instance, they'll stop at nothing. They'll assume you know something even if you don't – or at least that you might have some idea where to look."

I shut my eyes for a second or two. When I open them, Jack is watching me carefully. "But you don't know anything, right? About the drug?"

I stare back. "Why, exactly, are you asking?"

"No reason." He holds up his hands in a gesture of surrender. "I simply want to be sure where we stand."

I picture Lizzie's words unravelling on my laptop screen. *Stay away from Jack. He's bad news.*

"So tell me, Jack," I narrow my eyes at him, my expression icy, "why would Lizzie warn me away from you?"

His face squirms and he leans back in his seat. "I guess she's angry with me. Holds me responsible for getting everyone in so much trouble."

Only that doesn't explain why she left so suddenly, does it? Why she chose that precise moment to run away. I go over our last meeting in the cafe. I mean, everything he's just told me happened back in June – why did Lizzie wait till mid August to disappear?

Because she saw him. Jack.

I flash back to her face as she stared out the cafe window. Her expression. It wasn't anger, it was fear. She saw Jack and she panicked.

I lift my gaze to check him out. He's looking past me, into the pub, making sure of something. I study the line of his jaw, that small hairline scar, like the faint mark on the underside of a leaf.

What does Lizzie know about Jack? I wonder. Why does he scare her so much?

"So tell me," I ask, clearing my throat. He turns back to me. "How come you know all this?"

"What do you mean?"

"How do you know so much about this gang?"

Jack stretches out his legs and examines his feet. His black boots are damp around the toe, as if he's been walking across wet grass. His voice is quiet when he answers. "I used to be a member of the organization, if you see what I mean."

"You *worked* for them?"

He presses his lips together. "Only briefly. But long enough to understand that these are very bad people." His eyes meet mine. "That they'll do whatever it takes."

"Bad people? Like how?"

Jack rubs his nose. "The whole operation is run by an ex-con called Tommy Crace," he says, glancing around. "A petty thief and thug who did time for GBH. And a lot else besides. But rumour has it he's done worse than that, you know, since he got into the business – only the police have never been able to pin anything else on him. And that's just Tommy – some of the people who work for him are almost as bad."

I close my eyes briefly, then fix them on his. "You said you worked for this gang. So how do I know you still don't?"

"I left," he says simply.

"And they let you?" Somehow I'm thinking it isn't that easy.

"Nah," Jack sniffs, picking up the cigarette pack again and twirling it in his fingers. "Not exactly. I had to trade… offer them something in return."

"What?" I ask, before realizing I don't need a reply.

Jack gazes at me with an uncomfortable expression.

"So what were you planning to do?" My voice rises. "Steal those notes? Blackmail my brother? And Rob?"

He shakes his head again. "I was hoping, given time, I could persuade them. And I'd have made sure they did all right out of it. But then…"

"Then that girl died."

He nods. "I told them, the gang, our deal was off. That the stuff was dodgy."

"And?"

"Like I said. They don't take no for an answer."

I pause for a moment. "So where does that leave you?"

Jack swallows again. Takes a deep breath and peers at me with those ash-grey eyes.

"Probably in just as much shit as you."

24

thursday 8th september

I can't sleep. I'm lying in bed, staring into the darkness, going over and over it all in my head. It's as if I'm actually there, at the party, seeing the girl collapse, the lights of the ambulance, the urgency of the paramedics. Max's face stricken with grief and shock.

Did he go with her, to the hospital? I wonder. I like to think he did. I like to think he stayed with her till the end.

And then I relive, again and again, those few days my brother came home, to a family oblivious to everything that had happened. And him unable to tell us any of it.

Just leave me alone, Sarah.

It must have been agony. It must have been so lonely. My heart aches just thinking about it.

Because if what I'm going through is even half what Max endured, I can't imagine how he stood it. Though a part of me – a little part – can't help feeling he deserved to suffer. That poor girl, Anna. Dead because Max – my brainy, clever, fabulous brother – decided to do something epically, monumentally stupid.

Eventually I drop off for a few hours, waking to the noise of Mum making breakfast in the kitchen. I hear the toaster pop, the sound of the kettle boiling. I drag myself out of bed and join her downstairs.

Her gaze hovers over me. I must look terrible. I feel terrible – leaden, achey.

"You okay?" she asks, sitting at the table, taking a bite of toast.

I nod. "Rough night, that's all."

"You want to talk about it?" Mum gives me a smile.

I gaze at her. I desperately need to talk to someone – dealing with this alone is almost more than I can bear. I consider breaking down, offloading all of it. Savour the promise of relief, knowing that Mum would call Dad and he'd come straight home and sort everything out. Go to the police, get them to stop this gang. Make this nightmare end.

I nearly succumb to the temptation, but studying Mum's face I know it would kill her. It really would. However much I ache to talk, to tell her about Jack and Lizzie, to get the police involved, I can't. It'd all come out about Max and the drugs and what happened to his girlfriend, and I can't bring myself to do that to her. Or Dad.

They think it was just one of those things. Through the agony of the last three months, it's all they've had to hang on to – that Max's death was sheer bad luck. Something that couldn't be prevented.

How can I take that away from them?

"It's nothing," I make myself say. "A bit nervous about my audition."

"Not long to go. Next Saturday, isn't it?"

I nod, feeling sick at the thought. When I got back from meeting Jack yesterday, I was too stirred up to do my singing, and today I feel too rough to do anything.

I dig my fingers into the palms of my hands. *Don't think about that now,* I tell myself. *Concentrate on sorting this out.*

"I'm going out with Aunt Helen this morning," says Mum. "She's picking me up in an hour. We're going to that new garden centre near Milford."

I look at her in surprise. A few weeks ago she could barely drag herself out of bed.

"Great idea," I say, realizing I have one of my own.

Mum glances at the time. "Won't you be late for college? I can give you a lift if you like."

I shake my head. "No lessons till lunchtime," I lie. "You go ahead. I'll do some practice then walk in later."

I wait until Mum is safely packed off in Aunt Helen's car, then call the college. I know no one will answer during the busy morning period, so I leave a message reporting myself as ill. I'll fake a sick note and take it in tomorrow.

Then I dial Lizzie's phone. It goes straight into voicemail. I consider leaving a message, but remember what she said about being careful. Could the gang possibly hack into her mobile?

Lizzie's right. When we talk, it has to be face-to-face. Or at least on the phone.

I make another coffee and force myself to wait ten more minutes until I'm certain Mum's not coming back for any reason. I try Lizzie's mobile again, just in case, but it still clicks straight to voicemail. I want to scream with frustration. Why hasn't she rung me like she promised?

But the answer to that is not something I want to dwell on. I know now why she's run away.

I only hope she's run far enough.

Finishing my coffee, I get the garage key out of the shed and heave open the metal door. Pull it carefully shut behind me before switching on the light. The old fluorescent tube flickers, then finally blinks on.

Everything looks normal. The stack of dining room chairs we inherited from Gran. Dozens of cans of half-used paint lined up on shelves. A broken freezer Dad's been meaning to take to the dump for over a year now.

Clearly whoever broke into the house didn't come in here, I think, running my gaze across all the junk we've acquired over the years and imagining the mess they'd have made. I guess they didn't find the key or have time to break the door down. Or decided it was too risky – you can see the garage door from the road and there's a good chance they'd be spotted.

I pick my way past an old trestle table loaded with rolls of wallpaper to the three cardboard boxes stashed right at the back, concealed under a couple of picnic rugs. Dad hid them so Mum wouldn't notice them if she ever took it into her head to come in here.

I grab the first box and pull it out. Something grey streaks away from behind and I let out an involuntary squeal. A mouse.

Resisting the urge to bolt back into the daylight, I take a deep breath and slide my finger under the tape holding the lid in place. Inside lie several books. I glance at the titles.

Damn. The other library books – I'd forgotten all about them. I put them aside on the trestle table, peering into the box to see what's underneath. Folders stuffed with paper. Reams and reams of it.

I lift out a large ring binder and sit on one of the old dining chairs to look through it. Mostly essays and term papers, littered with diagrams and formulae. There's an occasional tick by the side of things Max wrote. The odd remark scrawled in red biro.

An interesting conclusion, I manage to make out, *but you'll need to justify why this doesn't result in a thermal...* I can't decipher the rest.

I lift out another folder. More of the same. Flicking through, I check each page as carefully as I can. Why didn't he write this stuff on his computer? I wonder, as I examine the familiar scrawl of Max's handwriting. He was the only person I knew who still used a fountain pen.

Further in the box are more books, one of them a novel. *Treasure Island* by Robert Louis Stevenson. Tucked inside the front cover is a photograph of Max and Rob and a girl I've never seen before. I stare at her wide smile, her deep brown hair, the dimples in her cheeks. She looks nice. Happy.

Is this Anna?

The thought pricks tears at my eyes. I think about the future Max and Anna could have had if this hadn't happened. They might have married. Had kids.

Or not. But even if the relationship hadn't gone anywhere, they would at least have still been alive.

I shiver, pulling my cardigan closer, then drag out the next box. Outside a siren blares past, making me jump with shock. I glance behind me, but the garage door remains firmly closed. *No one can get in,* I tell myself, *not without me hearing.*

The second box doesn't take long. It's crammed with Max's clothes – jeans, T-shirts, socks, underpants – all thrown in unfolded. I wonder if they're even clean. It feels weird, handling this stuff. Intrusive, too intimate. I have to push myself to check through it.

As I open the third box and rummage inside I hear the distant ring of the phone inside the house. I ignore it, pulling out a kettle and several mugs, one of them cracked. Judging by the careless way everything's been tossed in,

I'm guessing Max's housemates packed his things. Dad would have done it properly, wrapping the mugs in newspaper to stop them chipping.

I squint at what's left at the bottom. I can't see well in the dim light of the garage, so steel myself to reach in and feel inside. My hand touches something solid and I lift it out. Notebooks, small with black covers, held together with a rubber band. I go to release them, but at that instant the house phone rings again.

Perhaps it's Lizzie, it occurs to me with a rush of hope, and I grab the notebooks and leave.

When I've spoken to Dad and lied through my teeth and pretended everything's fine, I sit on my bed with Max's notebooks. I remove the rubber band and work through the first. It's full of lecture notes, from what I can tell, interspersed with hastily scribbled drawings. There's a molecule diagram with lines between various Hs and Cs and As. I turn it on its side – it looks a bit like the segments of a caterpillar.

I flick right through, trying to make some kind of sense of it all. *Substitution at Carbonyl Groups – Leaving Groups and Use of pKa as a Guide to the Breakdown of Tetrahedral Intermediates* reads one title. It might as well be written in a foreign language.

I turn the page. *CHECK OUT RATE OF POLYMERIZATION* Max has scrawled. I get up and type "polymerization" into Google and get lots of stuff about joining up molecules. Nothing looks out of the ordinary.

The second notebook contains much the same. And the third. My attention is flagging by the time I pick up the fourth and open it up to yet more diagrams, looking like pieces of broken honeycomb. A couple of pages on, Max has jotted a few words and underlined them – *recondensing* and *alternatives to the Ritter reaction?* followed by a list of chemicals with names like *3,4-methylenedioxyphenyl-2-propanone* and *toluene isopropyl alcohol*.

It's worth a try. I go back to my laptop, type in *ritter reaction*. All that comes up is lots of complicated stuff I can't be bothered to read. I tag *toluene isopropyl alcohol* onto the end in the search bar and press Enter.

A lump forms in my throat as I stare at the screen. Dozens of hits – most of them on manufacturing ecstasy.

Oh god…so it's true. What Jack told me is actually *true*.

Part of me was hoping he was lying. Or simply mistaken. I just hadn't wanted to believe it.

But here it is. No mistake. No mistake at all.

I flip through the remaining pages, not bothering to read more carefully. There's no way I can work out what's going on here.

As I get towards the end I see it. The ragged edge of paper where a number of pages were torn out together. And suddenly I know, with a sinking feeling of a plan in ruins, that these are the ones that matter. These are what that gang is looking for. What I was hoping might get us out of this mess.

The missing notes that are worth a fortune.

My only chance to end this once and for all.

25

"You're going to Sweden."

"Yes."

"To where Max…"

"Yes."

Jack sucks his teeth for a minute. He's perched on the swing, his hand in his pocket, fidgeting with the cigarette box. I've just told him I'm going to our summer house. That I want to see where Max died.

I'm hoping Jack will leave it at that.

I survey the park. It's only two days since we met in the pub, but already the world around us seems to be changing. Some of the trees have begun to shed their leaves. It's properly cold too, though it's only mid-September; I had to dig out a scarf from the back of the hall cupboard.

Maybe I should have suggested meeting somewhere warmer, some place indoors, but I wasn't thinking about the weather when I sent Jack the text. I simply picked somewhere public, somewhere I knew I'd be safe.

I'm still far from sure I can trust him.

"How long are you going for?" Jack asks.

"A few days."

His brow contracts in disapproval. "Sarah, you need to get away for more than—"

"How long are you saying I should disappear for, exactly?" I snap, my frustration spilling over. "Months? Years?"

He doesn't reply.

"I don't have months or years. I don't even have a week. I've got an audition next week – there's no way I'm going to miss that."

Jack looks at me. "Does it matter to you that much? Singing, I mean?"

I frown. How does he know it's for singing? Have I mentioned it before? Or did Max say something?

"Yes, it matters." I look at the ground, afraid I might cry. "It's everything, if you really want to know. If I can't do that, then…" I can't even finish the sentence.

Jack says nothing. I take a deep breath and turn to face him. "Anyway, you keep saying I should go away, but what could they actually *do*, this gang? They've already gone through our stuff. They know we've not got anything that interests them."

"That might only suggest they need to look harder." Jack shrugs. "Or that maybe they should take a shortcut."

"A shortcut?"

"Pay you a visit. Pick your brains, so to speak."

He says this in a way that makes my skin crawl. I don't even want to consider what he means.

"They might even decide they want to hang on to you. Use you to flush out Rob and your friend Lizzie."

"Take me hostage, you mean?"

"Kind of."

I stare at him, open-mouthed. Is he serious? I examine his face, searching for signs that he's joking.

I don't find any.

Oh god. And if they did get hold of me, would they ever let me go again? Could they risk it? I'm shivering, and it's not only the late afternoon chill. I've no idea whether this gang...this Tommy Crace...would go that far, but I'm sure I don't want to find out.

Jack eyes me carefully. "Sarah, I can't say what they'll do or how long you should stay away. I don't have all the answers. But don't you understand how much this is worth to them?"

I nod. I'm not going to try to put a figure on it, but I'm guessing it's a very big number.

"Listen to me," he says, glancing around again. "I know the lengths they'll go to when they want something this badly. They're like wolves, these people. They hunt you down till they get what they're after."

I feel my breath catch but don't let my anxiety show.

"Face it, right now you're the best lead they've got."

"What about my parents?" I ask, voicing the concern that's haunted me since our last meeting.

Jack looks at his feet. "I don't think they'd bother with them. They know that if your mum and dad were in any way involved, they'd have gone to the police. Besides, what kid ever tells their parents anything? They can be pretty sure Max didn't drag them into it."

I let his words sink in. Feel a small measure of relief.

"But I can't simply up and disappear for good," I say quietly, kicking at a stone under my swing. "I can't give up college and my music and everything. I can't do that to my parents – not after what happened with Max."

Jack ponders this for a while. "So why go at all?"

"I don't know. I just feel I have to."

It's not the whole truth, but it's a big part of it. I want to piece together what happened to my brother. To make sense of something that right now feels pretty senseless.

"So what are you going to tell your parents? About going away, I mean."

"My dad's not here. He's working on an oil rig and there's been a lot of problems, so I doubt he'll be home before I get back. And I've managed to persuade Mum to go off for a few days."

It's taken some doing. I had to ring Aunt Helen and get her to suggest it, or else Mum would be suspicious. Luckily they both decided it was a brilliant idea. "Exactly what your mum needs," Aunt Helen said. "Bit of a holiday. We might go down to Totnes, where we used stay when we were little. She's always saying she wants to go back."

Which is perfect, I now realize. If Jack's wrong, if the gang do decide to target my parents, they won't be easy to find. They'll be safe for as long as this will take.

So all I have to do now is fake another sick note for school. Say I need some time off on compassionate grounds, something like that.

"You planning to go on your own?" Jack asks.

I nod.

He leans back, elbows crooked round the chains holding up the swing, and gazes up into the clouds high above our heads. "I should come with you," he says finally.

I shake my head. "No."

He drops his gaze to mine. "So when are you leaving?"

"Tomorrow."

Jack lifts his eyebrows in surprise.

"Like I said," I shrug, "I've got to get back soon."

"For your audition?"

I nod. Six days. It's enough. Six days to get there, find what I hope I'll find, and get back. Just in time for my big day on Saturday.

It means cancelling a session with Mrs Perry, but I'll have to live with that. I'll text her en route. Pretend I've got a headache or something.

Jack carries on gazing at me. Thinking. "Are you going to tell me why you want to go to Sweden?" he asks after a minute or so. "It's a bit gruesome, isn't it?"

"I can't explain. It just feels important." I hold his gaze, resisting the urge to blink. I've no intention of telling him more than I absolutely have to.

"You still don't trust me, do you?"

I let my silence serve as an answer.

Jack sighs. "I guess I can't blame you." He twists his swing round so it's facing me. "But listen, let me come with you. It's not right, you going all that way on your own. And I can be there…just in case…"

"Just in case what?"

He rubs his nose. "You know. In case you run into any kind of trouble."

I feel a hot flush of anxiety. "You don't think they'd follow me up there? I mean, how would they know? They're not watching me, are they?" I glance about quickly.

Nothing but playing fields and trees. A few people walking dogs. A gang of kids kicking a football while their parents look on.

"I'm not sure," Jack says. "I don't think so. They generally stick to their own patch. I haven't seen anyone about, certainly not Tommy or Kev or any of the other blokes I know. But I still reckon you shouldn't go alone."

"Why do you care?"

Jack kicks at the ground, frustration all over his face. "Look, Sarah, I told you. I've been watching out for you. I'm trying to *protect* you."

"But why?" I persist. "*Why* do you care so much what happens to me? Is it just guilt or what?"

He stays silent for a moment, then his shoulders slump downwards.

"Guilt, yeah. And I guess you remind me of someone."

"Who?"

Jack looks away. "My sister."

A pang of something I can't define. "You have a sister?"

He nods. "Yeah. Younger than me. A bit younger than you too. She still lives with my mum and my stepfather."

I study his face. "How old are you anyway?"

"Twenty-three."

He looks older somehow. Like he's lived through more than his years.

"Do you see her?"

"Who?"

"Your sister."

His face clouds. That twitch in the corner of his eye. "Not often. I had to go away for a while and afterwards he…my stepdad…didn't want me near her."

I can imagine. What father wants a drug dealer around his daughter?

There's a tightness in his jaw and his throat moves as he swallows. "I used to go to her school sometimes, stand outside the playground, just to check she was okay. That's when I saw him…one of the pushers from the gang, hanging about, trying to get in with the older kids."

He stares off towards the cricket pavilion, then looks round at me. "That's when I knew I had to get out."

I gaze back at him, trying to see past those ash-grey eyes and fathom what sort of person lies behind.

But all I see is myself. My own face, reflected in his.

Should I trust Jack? I wonder again. How do I know he's telling the truth about any of this? How can I be sure he's no longer working for these people?

Perhaps I really should go to the police. Tell them everything. Let them handle it. God knows I've come close a dozen times this past week.

I remind myself why I've held back – it would all come out, and Mum and Dad would find out about Max. I couldn't bear that, not when Mum seems to be emerging from that dark hole she fell into after his death.

I inhale deeply, tasting the cold, evening air. Admit to myself that there's another reason. One I've grappled with over and over. I'd have to tell the police everything I know about Jack – and somehow I'm thinking that wouldn't work out so well for him.

Because the truth is I want to believe what he's said. That he's been looking out for me, keeping me safe. And that he wants out. So how can I walk into a police station and dump him in it?

I gaze towards the clumps of trees lining the river. A pair of dogs are racing about, chasing each other as their owners watch. It's so normal, so ordinary, that I have to look away. I feel outside all that now – the everyday stuff going on around me. It all feels a million miles away.

If I turn Jack in, I'll be in this alone. And if what he's told me about this drug gang is true, getting the police involved wouldn't be the end of my problems. Because Jack said, didn't he, that they haven't been able to pin much on this Tommy guy. And what proof do I have of anything? Nothing that would convince the police that we require protection.

I need Jack, I realize. He's the only person who knows who these people are, what they're truly capable of.

I turn to look at him, but he's facing away from me now, gazing into the distance, his black hair a little wind-blown, a faint shadow along his jawline, like he forgot to shave. Even at rest, he exudes a tight, taut energy, an agitation that never seems to subside. Always alert. Always watchful.

When your life is in danger, I think, who do you really want on your side? Someone good, someone decent, someone who only ever does the right thing?

Couldn't the opposite be true? What if, when your world grows dark, you're better off with someone who's lived in the shadows? Someone who's seen and done things you can't even imagine. Someone who's prepared to do whatever it takes.

Maybe, when your life threatens to collapse beneath you, the only person who can help is the last person on earth you should actually trust.

sunday 11th september

I stare at the car. It's an old Ford Fiesta, a hatchback with a big door in the boot and a black plastic trim. The kind of car Aunt Helen might drive.

I can't stop myself. I do the last thing I thought I'd be capable of right now. I start laughing.

Jack looks annoyed. "What's so funny?"

"Your car."

"What's wrong with it?"

"Nothing. It's just not the sort I'd expect a drug dealer to drive."

"I've told you, I don't deal any—"

Another fit of giggles. I run my hand along the dark green paintwork. "I mean, it's not very gangsta, is it?"

Jack's scowl morphs into a smile. "What makes you think I haven't got a Maserati tucked away in a lock-up somewhere? Anyway, the whole point is not to draw attention to ourselves."

I grin. It feels like the first time in for ever I haven't had to force one.

"Besides," Jack sniffs, "it's not mine. It belongs to a friend."

"What about your SUV?"

"I borrowed this instead."

I don't ask him why. I have a horrible feeling I know the answer. To throw *them* off our track. Clearly he's more worried about them following us than he's letting on.

He grabs my holdall and flings it in the back. Then opens the passenger door for me with a little bow, like a chauffeur. I can't help smiling again.

My good mood lasts for as long as it takes for him to climb into the driving seat. I do up my seat belt, praying he'll start the engine before I change my mind. About going, about letting Jack come with me. About everything.

It's still not too late, says a voice in my head. *You don't have to do this. You can go on your own.*

But the truth is I'm far more scared than I'm willing to admit. And when it comes down to it, I'm not sure I can handle travelling all that way alone. Because, if what Jack said about these people is true, there *is* a risk they might follow me. And if they did, would I stand a chance on my own?

No, I think. No chance at all.

Better the devil you know and all that.

So I sit and wait for Jack to drive off, but he's resting both arms on the steering wheel, staring at the road ahead. I'm not the only one having second thoughts, I realize.

"Are you really sure about this, Sarah? Wouldn't it make more sense to join your friend or something?"

I pick at my nail. It's not like I haven't considered it.

I'm certain if I put enough pressure on Lizzie, I could get her to tell me where she is. Or at least agree to meet me.

But either way, as a plan, it has one flaw. A big one. When would we ever come home again? From what Jack told me, this gang won't give up so easily. I imagine they're perfectly prepared to bide their time.

So that would be it. We couldn't come back. Probably not for months. Years even. And what would I tell Mum and Dad? What about college?

My audition?

No, there's only one way I'm going to get them off our backs. Make us all safe again.

And that's to give them exactly what they want.

27

sunday 11th september

It's turned sunny, one of those hot days you sometimes get in September, like the last gasp of summer. Jack's car hasn't got air conditioning, and it smells funny, so I open my passenger window and let the fresh breeze blast in.

As we pull on to the ring road that leads to the motorway I'm almost enjoying myself. I always loved travelling, even as a kid. Not the arriving, but the process of getting there. There's something about moving from one place to another that makes you feel suspended, as if all your problems have receded to the margins and you can simply enjoy the ride.

Most people moan about long journeys; right now I'm thinking the longer the better. I'm dreading arriving in Sweden. Dreading what I might have to deal with there.

And just as worried I may find nothing at all.

Up ahead the traffic slows for roadworks. I stare out the window while Jack fiddles with the satnav he's plugged into the car's cigarette lighter. We're down to a few miles an hour now, inching past houses and fields at barely more than a walking pace.

I find I'm checking out the vehicles around us, wondering who might be in them. I'm half tempted to ask Jack more about this gang, what they look like, what kind of car they'd drive, but stop myself. What's the point in making myself any more paranoid?

I have to trust that Jack knows what he's doing. After all, he's already swapped his car. He's clearly given this some thought.

We crawl towards an office building faced with a line of trees and bushes running parallel to the road. I notice several squat little plants, studded with bright blue flowers. I crane my head to gaze at them as we pass.

"Ceratostigma," Jack says.

"Cerato-what?"

"That shrub. It's called ceratostigma."

I turn and stare at him. "How do you even know that?"

He shrugs. "I had a Saturday job for a while in the local garden centre. You pick things up."

"You're kidding."

He looks at me as the traffic slows almost to a halt. "No, as it happens. I was well into it. Considered going to college, you know, to study horticulture. Before my stepdad…" His face darkens and his eyelid flutters momentarily, as if warding off a memory. "Anyway, I always wanted to go back to it. Maybe train up in garden maintenance or design or something."

I can't help it. I snort with laughter.

Jack looks over with a slightly hurt expression. "That funny, huh, Chicory?"

"You're having me on, aren't you?"

His features tighten. "Of course. Because I'm, what… just some lowlife who enjoys winding you up?"

"I didn't mean—"

"You're not the only one who wants to do something with their life. Make a go of things."

"I'm sorry," I say, meaning it.

Jack runs his tongue over his teeth and falls silent. Just taps a beat on the steering wheel. I let it go on for a minute or two before I speak.

"Anyway, what's with the chicory? Why call me that?"

This time it's Jack who laughs. When he doesn't answer I kick off my boots and put my feet up on the dashboard. Pull out my phone.

Still nothing from Lizzie, despite the text I sent telling her I was going away. I didn't say where. I thought it best not to. In case anyone has access to her phone.

A pang of guilt as I remember Lizzie's mum and my promise to let her know if I heard anything. I should have called. But what would I tell her? What on earth could I say that wouldn't make her ten times more anxious?

I'll deal with it when I get back, I tell myself. When maybe I'll have made this whole thing go away.

"Jeez," mutters Jack, eyeing the swathe of orange cones extending for what looks like miles up the centre of the carriageway.

I close my eyes and settle back in my seat. Am nearly drifting off when my phone gives a single short bleep. When I check it, the screen is blank. What the hell? I only charged it a few hours ago.

I give it a shake. Nothing. Press the start button and after a few seconds, the screen fires up again.

Bloody phone. Now and then it plays up, but never enough for me to bother replacing it.

Jack leans over and turns on the radio with his left hand. Rap thumps out of the speakers. I suppress a smile. True to type there, at least.

But as we get past the roadworks and speed on towards the motorway, I'm becoming more and more uneasy. Am I mad, doing this? With this guy who has more secrets than I'll ever know?

I sneak a look at him out the corner of my eye. He's got his window down, his right arm resting on the sill, his fingers drumming time on the car door. The air rushing in is blowing his hair around his face, making his features appear softer somehow. I watch him and feel a rush of something. Gratitude, maybe.

Because I know it's not only me taking a risk. Jack clearly has a lot to lose by hanging out with me. How can he be sure I won't just walk into the next police station and dump him in it?

After all, when he told me about his sister, about going away, I had a good idea where he'd been.

And I doubt it's anywhere he's keen to get back to.

28

sunday 11th september

I wake with a start to the screech of car tyres. Ours, I grasp, as I see we're no longer on the M25, but hurtling around the backstreets of some strange town.

"Where are we?"

Jack doesn't answer. He's watching the road with fierce concentration as he pulls right into another street so sharply that I'm flung against the passenger door, knocking my elbow. The cigarette box on the dashboard shoots into my lap.

"Jesus!" I yelp, rubbing my arm.

But Jack ignores me. He's accelerating forwards, at the same time staring into his rear-view mirror. I turn and look out the back windscreen, but can't see anything out of the ordinary.

"Keep your head down!" he barks, and I duck instinctively.

Jack turns left with another squeal from the tyres and pulls behind a white van parked by the kerb. He sinks low into his seat, his eyes fixed on his side mirror.

I try to steady my breathing. "What's going on?"

He doesn't reply, just carries on monitoring the road behind us. A green Clio drives past, followed by a black SUV.

"Jack?"

He turns round and looks out the rear window, then slumps back with a sigh.

"I thought we were being followed," he says quietly, his eyes fixed on the wing mirror.

"Really?"

"I'm not sure. Maybe."

I feel my pulse start to race. I have to make a conscious effort to keep breathing.

"Anyhow, if that was them, I think we've shaken them off." He sits back up and turns the keys in the ignition, pulling out into the road and heading back the way we came.

My hand is shaking as I lean forward and pick the pack of cigarettes from my lap. I've never smoked before, but I'm figuring now might be a good time to start. I open the lid, but there's nothing inside.

"You're out." I hold up the box so he can see it's empty.

"I know."

I chuck it back on the dashboard and glance at Jack. It occurs to me that I've never actually seen him smoking.

He meets my gaze. "I gave up a few years ago, but I missed having something to keep my hands busy. And, I dunno, having the box reminds me…"

"Of what?"

"Not to slip up again."

I think about this until I see, several miles later, the signs to Colchester. "Where are we going?" I'd assumed we were heading for Dover, to get the ferry to France and then drive north. More or less the way I'd have gone by train.

"Change of plan, Chicory." Jack's voice is curt, decisive, and I decide it's best not to ask why. I have the feeling he knows what he's doing.

"We can get a boat from Harwich straight across to Denmark," he says. "It'll cost more, but I'd rather spend less time on the road."

"Okay."

I wait a full half-hour before I tell him I need the loo. He pulls up at the next services without a word and I jump out and head into the building. He locks the car behind us and trails me across the car park.

"Five minutes," he says, before disappearing into the cafe.

When I get back, Jack's already sitting in the driving seat. He tosses a packet of sandwiches at me as I climb in. I peer through the cellophane. Cheese and ham, oozing mayonnaise. I put them back in the little space in front of the gearstick.

"It's all they had," Jack says. "You can always take out the ham." He looks tired and cross, the lighter mood of earlier turned dark and sour.

I shake my head. "I'm not that hungry."

"Fair enough." He gives me a funny look, then picks up the packet and rips it open, devouring the first sandwich in a couple of wolfish bites. I can hardly believe how fast it disappears.

As he gets out to dispose of the wrappers, his mobile drops out of his pocket. I hand it back when he returns. "Why so old school?" I ask, nodding at it. "You wouldn't need to draw maps if you had a smart phone."

"Keep it simple," he sniffs. "I'm not keen on too much technology, leaving traces of yourself everywhere. Basic phone, one that doesn't break easily, and pay-as-you-go – that's your safest bet."

I consider this as we head off eastwards, wondering if I should switch off mine. Could this gang, this Tommy and his crew, pick up its signal? Use it to trace us? After all, it's a fair assumption that they know my number.

Surely not, I conclude. I'm pretty certain only the police can do that. I'm about to ask Jack when he pulls off the main road and heads into the centre of town.

"Harwich isn't this way, is it?" I say, confused.

"I know. I'm taking the scenic route."

Jack drives through the town centre and onto the road signposted to Ipswich, turning off after a couple of miles into a country lane. He pulls up in the gateway of a field, and we sit there for five minutes, the engine idling.

"What are we doing?" I ask, when Jack doesn't offer any explanation.

"Just checking." He pulls back into the road and heads deeper into the countryside, following the satnav north. It takes ages. Most of the lanes are too narrow for two cars, so we're always having to pull over to let people pass. Several times we have to back up for a tractor.

Eventually we emerge onto the main road and this time Jack follows the signs for the ferry terminal. A few minutes later we arrive.

"What was that all about?" I ask as we pull up outside the ticket office. "Back there. Do you still think we're being followed?"

Jack shakes his head as he releases his seat belt and climbs out the car. "I don't reckon so. But you can never be too careful."

Maybe I'm going about this all wrong, I worry, as he disappears into the building. Maybe I should get in contact with this gang, tell them I'll cooperate, will get them what they want.

I close my eyes, trying to rub away the tension in my forehead. But what if I don't find those notes? What then? They don't seem the kind to accept failure lightly.

I feel another lurch of panic.

No, I decide, opening my eyes again and letting the world drift back into focus. I have to do this on my own terms.

Keep my options open.

* * *

Jack's gone for twenty minutes or so, then returns clutching a printout and hands me my passport. We join the line of cars waiting to embark.

Jack tilts his seat back and leans along it. He closes his eyes, and I can see how tired he is, noticing for the first time the dark hollows around his cheeks. I let my eyes linger on the scar on his lip, wondering again how he got it, and can't help thinking he's quite nice-looking in a scruffy, careless sort of way.

I swing my gaze up to the big white ship, hung with three small lifeboats. *DFDS Seaways*, it says on the side in large blue lettering. It's much bigger than I imagined. At least seven decks, counting the rows of little round portholes.

A man approaches and taps on the window, his hand held out for our ticket. Jack jumps at the sound, his eyes blinking open. He winds down his window and passes it over. The man scans it briefly before nodding and pointing towards customs.

We drive through slowly, Jack's eyes fixed on the lane ahead. But as one of the customs officers raises his palm for us to stop, I see the tendons in his neck go rigid. His jaw is tight as he lowers his window again.

The customs officer nods at Jack then peers into the car, looking briefly at me then across to the back seat. I feel a twinge of embarrassment – he must be assuming we're together.

"Would you mind stepping out for a minute, Sir?"

As Jack reaches to open the door I notice that twitch again in his left eye. A tiny flicker, there for a moment, then gone. Jack appears almost relaxed as he gets out the car, casting a friendly smile at the customs man.

"Could I ask you to open the boot?" The man addresses Jack with a face devoid of expression, observing him carefully as he walks round and swings up the back of the car.

I see Jack eyeing the large black dog, held on a leash by another customs officer, a woman about Mum's age, with a demeanour as blank as her colleague's. She brings it over and it sniffs the air around the boot as the customs man leans in and sifts through our bags. Jack stands watching, his hands tucked casually into the front pockets of his jeans, only he's standing more stiffly than usual. Uneasy.

"That's fine, Sir."

The customs officer gestures for Jack to close the boot before ambling back round to the open window. He glances at the back seat again before his eyes rest on me.

"Have a nice journey, Miss." He smiles, and retreats to the white booth a few metres up ahead.

Jack climbs back into his seat, leaning across me to throw his passport and the ticket into the glove compartment. I can hear a slight catch in his breathing, see his skin has lost its colour.

He's hiding something, I realize. Something he's scared they would find.

Neither of us speaks as we drive up the ramp and into the bowels of the boat, and all I can think is that I have just made the worst mistake of my life.

29

sunday 11th september

I follow Jack into the cafeteria on the main deck of the boat. He joins the end of the queue, ordering a plate of chips with two dense-looking sausages.

"You want some?" He nods at his food as he sits at an empty table. It's nearly six and the place is already filling with people, most of them speaking Danish or another Scandinavian-sounding language.

I shake my head. "I told you. I don't eat meat."

"Why not?"

"I gave it up years ago, when I was around ten or eleven. It just freaked me out somehow, the thought of eating something that had been alive."

Jack lifts an eyebrow. "So what exactly do you eat, Chicory?" His tone mocking.

I ignore him, turning to look out the window at the receding coastline. The sun is setting, lighting up the distant fields with a warm golden glow. A sudden rush of homesickness threatens to overwhelm me and I have to blink hard for a minute to clear my vision.

What the hell am I doing here?

I take a deep breath and walk up to the counter. Buy myself a cheese roll, a packet of crisps and a can of Coke. I return to Jack's table and hold out my hand. "Can I have the room key?"

He fishes in his pocket, still chewing on a lump of sausage, and pulls out a plastic card. I make my way down to the bottom deck and let myself into the cabin, turning on the light.

A loo and shower are tucked into a tiny bathroom just inside the door. There's no porthole – only a couple of dim lamps on the wall. The whole place is claustrophobically small, about the size of our garden shed, though at least it's clean and has no cobwebs.

But there are two bunks. And I'm guessing Jack only booked one cabin.

The thought of sleeping in the same room as him makes me feel almost feverish with discomfort. I toy with the idea of going upstairs and seeing if I can find a reclining chair to spend the night in.

Sod it. I'm too tired. I flop onto the bottom bunk, pull my music out of my rucksack and put in my earphones. Try to do some practice. The walls are thin, so all I can do is hum through the pieces, checking my timing, trying to get the right emphasis on each note. It's better than nothing, but I know I should be exercising my voice, strengthening it in time for the audition.

It'll have to wait, I think, unwrapping the bread roll and chewing it slowly. I'll have to find another opportunity.

At least I've got some time on my own. Time to sort things out a bit in my head.

But my mind keeps conjuring up Jack's face as we went through customs. The twitch in his eye that gave him away – at least to me.

Jack has something to hide, I'm certain. And you don't need to be a genius to work out what.

The boat begins to pitch and sway as soon as we leave the shelter of the harbour, until my head and stomach are filled with a terrible draggy feeling. I'm glad of the crisps. I prop myself up with the pillow and nibble at them one by one, the saltiness making me feel a little better.

Nearly an hour after we set sail my phone rings. I grab it out my pocket and look at the screen. Caller number unknown.

I accept the call.

"Sarah?" The voice sounds distant and crackly, but I recognize it immediately.

"Lizzie…is that you?"

A blast of static. I check the signal strength on my mobile – only one bar. Damn. We must be getting too far from land.

"I got your text. Sarah, listen, there's some stuff I've really got to tell you. I'm so sorry, I should have said something before but…" Her voice fades for a few seconds, and I'm not sure whether it's her or the connection.

"Lizzie, look I know about—"

"...there's things I have to tell you, about the party, and that man who..."

"I know," I say quickly. "I know all about it. And Rob too. That you're with him. It's a bit late, though, isn't it, Lizzie?" My voice starting to rise. "Why didn't you tell me before? Warn me about all the shit we were in?"

I can't hide the hurt, the sense of betrayal. "I mean, what the hell, Lizzie? What were you thinking?"

A silence at the other end of the line. For a moment I think she's rung off. Then a strangled, anguished sound. I can tell she's crying.

"I'm so, so sorry," she sobs. "You're right, of course you're right. I didn't tell you about Rob cos...well...I wasn't sure how you'd react and I didn't even know there was anything real there and then when I did...well..."

"It happened," I fill in. "With Max's girlfriend."

Lizzie sniffs. "I wanted to talk to you, Sarah. Really. Every day I thought about telling you. Every single day, but..." Her voice chokes. Stops.

"It's all right," I say, my anger dying away as suddenly as it arose. "I understand. I understand why you couldn't tell me that about Max."

It's true. I know Lizzie couldn't face telling me about Max any more than I can face telling Mum or Dad what's going on. Or Lizzie's mum, for that matter.

And even if she had, even if Lizzie had found the courage to let me know my brother made a drug that killed

218

a girl, would I even have believed her?

"I thought if I went away, it would take the heat off," Lizzie explains, her voice mournful. "Maybe they'd come looking for me. Leave you alone."

I don't know what to say to that. Clearly that wasn't much of a plan. Another few seconds of silence, then I hear Lizzie draw in a breath. "Look, I'll talk to Rob. I'll persuade him to come back with me and go to the poli...just don't..." She dissolves into crackle.

"Lizzie?"

"Sarah...Sarah? I can't hear..." Her voice cuts in, then breaks up into syllables. I can't understand anything she's saying.

"Lizzie, I'll call you when I get there, when I've got a better signal."

"Get where? Sarah, where exactly are you going?" Her words are clear again for a few seconds, the alarm in them unmistakable.

"I'm going to Sweden, Lizzie. I'm going to try and sort all this out."

More crackling, then Lizzie again, fainter now. "...shit...I can't hear..." I can't make out the words, only the desperation in her tone. "...Sarah, you need to go home. You don't under...just stay away from Ja..."

"What? Lizzie? What did you say?"

The line goes dead. I'm talking to myself.

I look at my phone. The screen is blank again. Hell. I scrabble for my charger in my bag and plug it in. Press the power button and wait for it to fire up. But nothing happens. I wait a couple more seconds then press it again. This time the screen lights up briefly, before reverting to a lifeless black.

Great. I fling it onto the end of the bed and lie back, closing my eyes in a bid to quell my rising sense of anxiety. What was Lizzie trying to say?

I steady my breathing and make myself think calmly. Lizzie warned me away from Jack before. She met him at that party and she clearly thinks he's dangerous. Maybe I should have told her he left that gang. Put her mind at ease.

The moment I consider it I know what she'd say. Or rather what she'd ask: *How can you be sure?*

And she'd be right. I mean, what do I really know about him besides what he's told me? I only have his word for any of it.

My mind goes back again to the scene at customs. Why was he so nervous? What had he got to hide?

The answer is obvious. Okay, the dog didn't pick up anything, but that's hardly surprising. After all, Jack's a drug dealer. He knows what he's doing, how to conceal things properly.

Outside the cabin the brief sound of a voice, then someone knocks loudly on the door. I freeze. For a second I think it must be him, before remembering Jack has another key card.

I lie still, holding my breath, feeling like something trapped, caught in a lair.

A minute later the knock comes again. Harder, this time, more insistent.

I don't move. I don't breathe. I just wait.

Finally, after what feels like an age, I hear the sound of footsteps retreating along the corridor.

I need him, I remind myself. Jack. He may be bad, he may be the last person on earth I should trust, he may be hiding something dodgy, but right now he's the only option I've got.

30

monday 12th september

I wake up fully clothed, my mouth tasting furry and stale from falling asleep without cleaning my teeth. I stumble out of bed, glancing up at the top bunk. There's no sign of it having been slept in, the thin blue duvet still smooth and taut, and the pillow lying perfectly square at the end.

I forage in my bag for my toothbrush and go into the bathroom, careful to lock the door. I brush my teeth and strip off, setting the shower to hot. Stand there for five minutes, letting the water scald me clean, then dress quickly, worried Jack might turn up at any moment.

In the end I have to go and look for him. I find him in the cafe, reading a paper over a cup of coffee. He looks awful, his eyes ringed with the colour of a fresh bruise and his hair sticking up at an angle.

He lifts an eyebrow as I approach. "Sleep okay?"

I nod, but it isn't true. I tossed and turned with each pitch and roll of the boat, churning over Lizzie's words. Waiting for the sound of Jack's key card in the door.

And trying to work out how I'd actually feel if I heard it.

"What happened to you?" I ask, sitting in the chair

opposite. I eye the coffee. It looks as thick and dark as treacle, but all the same I'm tempted.

Jack squints at me.

"You didn't come back to the room," I say.

He grimaces. "No."

"Why not?"

I'm not sure why I'm asking. I'm not sure why I even want to know.

He shrugs. "Small cabins. I don't like confined spaces."

"You're claustrophobic?"

"Not exactly."

"What then?"

"Jesus, Sarah, what's this about?" His mouth narrows in annoyance. "Miss me that much, did you?"

I feel my cheeks flush and I look away.

"Okay," Jack sighs, a few moments later. "If you really want to know, I did time. You know, prison. Those little cabins, they remind me of cells."

That shuts me up. I stare out the window at the horizon for a full five minutes. We're still out in open water, the waves sloshing and churning as far as I can see.

I turn back to him. "What was it like?"

"What?"

"Prison."

Jack picks up his coffee and downs it in one gulp. "Believe me, Chicory, you really don't want to know."

* * *

223

It takes us half an hour to disembark at Esjberg, which sounds like "iceberg" when they announce our arrival in Danish. This time customs is no more than a quick flick through our passports. Jack hands both ours over with an easy smile.

"Where are you heading?" the man asks in nearly accentless English.

"Norway." Jack doesn't even blink as he says it.

The customs man waves us through and we head into the town, which from the outskirts doesn't look much different from the back end of anywhere at home. But as we pull out into the countryside Denmark reveals itself as a flat sort of place, endless fields of grass and naked earth surrounded by long, grey expanses of horizon.

The largest things on the landscape are the pylons and the wind turbines. There are lots of windmills, tall and graceful. Three ahead of us seem almost to hover over the road, blades rotating in unison. I can't tear my eyes from them; there's something mesmeric in their slow rhythm, like a silent metronome.

A few drops of rain spatter on the windscreen. Jack swears as someone cuts him up on the motorway – a big black BMW with a couple of kayaks on top. Going on holiday, I think enviously, unable now to imagine ever being that carefree. Having a life where enjoying yourself is even an option.

I rest my head on the side window, letting the scenery blur into streaks of green and grey. Wasn't that TV show set in Denmark? The one I watched with Mum a couple of years ago, where the girl vanishes and they find her body in the boot of a car. I shiver as I remember it. She can't have been much older than me.

Pull yourself together, I think, lifting my head and focusing on a group of squat little houses huddling between the fields. This doesn't seem the kind of place girls get themselves murdered.

Another hour passes. Jack drives at a steady seventy-five, never exceeding the speed limit. I keep my gaze fixed outside, trying to remember if I've ever travelled this particular route before. Maybe when I was little. But I haven't been to the summer house since I was twelve, and that time we flew straight into Gothenburg.

A dark green car edges past us in the left-hand lane, with a dog and two small kids in the back. I glance at the number plate. British. A pang of homesickness ripples through me, and I keep my head turned away so Jack can't see my face.

"You okay?" he asks, after ten more minutes of flat landscape.

"Just tired," I say, and he nods.

Up ahead I spot a little picture of an aeroplane and the word *Bilund* underneath, though I'm not sure if that's a name or Danish for airport. Did Max read this too, I wonder, cross these same miles of tarmac on his way north?

I doubt it. Max couldn't drive, and he didn't like planes, so he probably took the train. It's one of those details that got lost in the aftermath, along with what he was doing at the summer house in the first place. We assumed he'd gone there to recover from his finals. To get away from it all.

Though not in the sense I now know to be true.

Now I understand what was really going on with him, I find myself imagining every mile of that long journey north and my heart aches with a fierce, sharp kind of pain. Did Max know it might well be his last trip? Did he have any idea that he'd never come home again?

Or was he, like me, simply hoping everything would somehow work out all right in the end?

Jack pulls off into a service station. Slams the car door and trudges into the shop. Several minutes later he's back, tossing me an unappetizing wedge of cheese and tomatoes sandwiched between slices of dark, almost black bread. I accept it graciously, but the whole thing tastes more of salt than anything else. It's a struggle to force half of it down.

"All I could find," Jack says, not even bothering to check out my expression. "Unless you're going to become a carnivore."

He finishes his sandwich in a few mouthfuls and sets off. The clouds are lower now, and Jack mutters as the rain intensifies, his face pale and tired. He pumps up the wiper speed, but doesn't slow down.

Kobenhavn says the sign overhead. *Copenhagen*, I translate in my mind, and soon a wide expanse of water opens up on my left, clutches of wind turbines visible on the other side of the bay. Ten minutes later we're on the Øresund Bridge that stretches between Denmark and Sweden, an endless, elegant sweep of road suspended just above the sea.

A line from *The Great Gatsby* pops into my mind, back from when we were studying it in Year Ten. *Anything can happen now that we've slid over this bridge. Anything at all.* A feeling of foreboding, deep inside, as I wonder if this is some kind of omen.

"Five miles long," Jack says as we head towards the enormous central pillars, and though I'm amazed he knows that, I don't say so. Just keep my eyes fixed on the giant metal sails topped with flashing lights that mark the mid-point of the bridge.

Sverige announces a blue sign. Sweden.

A few minutes later we're approaching Malmö, and Jack shoves a handful of notes at me when we reach the toll. I wind down the window and hand them to the man in the booth, who smiles and gives half of them back, along with a receipt.

Nearly three hundred Danish kroner. How much is that? I work it out. About thirty pounds. Jeez. All this is costing far more than I imagined. I should give Jack some money, I think, but when I tried to pay him for the boat ticket he refused. He could afford it more than me, he said.

But how?

You know how, says a voice in my head, but it's not one I want to listen to right now. So I push the thought from my mind and sit in silence as Jack drives into the centre of Malmö. We don't hang around. I only have time to dive into a coffee shop and get us both a cardboard cup full of strong, black coffee while he goes to the cashpoint to get some Swedish kronor.

A shaft of sunlight breaks through the clouds as we head up the coastline, illuminating the waves and the distant chimneys barely visible across the water. My heart lifts a little at the sight of it.

Jack fiddles with the radio, but all the stations are in Swedish, or playing music he clearly doesn't like. He clicks it off in disgust.

"Talk to me, Sarah."

I turn to look at him. "What about?"

"Anything. Just help me stay awake."

I rack my brains for something to say. There are so many things we can talk about – and so many things we can't – that I draw a blank.

"Your sister," I venture finally. "What's she like?"

The moment I ask I regret it. I see Jack's jaw tense, his hands clenching on the steering wheel, as if riding out a wave of physical pain.

"Not much to say," he replies after a pause. "She's an ordinary kid."

"What's her name?"

"Phoebe."

"What does she want to do?"

Jack's mouth lifts into a smile. I can tell he's picturing her now. Remembering something she said. "She wants to be a marine biologist."

"Really?" I say. "Wow!"

Max wanted to be a research chemist. The kind that works on new drugs, discovering ways to cure people, to make them better. I close my eyes briefly. The irony isn't lost on me.

"Ever since I took her to the aquarium," Jack says. "You know, the big one down in Southampton. She decided that's what she wants to do."

I smile too. She sounds nice. "I can tell you're proud of her."

Jack nods. Overtakes a lorry in the slow lane. "She works hard, determined to do well in her exams. And she will." He glances over at me. "She's like you – gritty, single-minded."

Like me? I'm not sure how to respond to that. Is that really how Jack sees me?

"She wants to go to university. Get on a good course. She's got her head screwed on right."

"So you have different dads?" I ask. "Your mum remarried, you said."

Jack's eye twitches. Again the sense that I've gone too far. "My real dad died when I was three. Had a brain aneurysm.

Dropped down dead at work, apparently. I can hardly remember him."

"But you don't get on with your stepdad?"

A sharp intake of breath. "No."

"Cos of the drugs?" I add before I can stop myself.

Jack doesn't respond for a minute. Then snorts. "Like he can talk. He drinks like a bloody drain, but according to him that's different." There's no missing the contempt in his voice. "Booze is legal. Which makes it okay, I guess, to slap people around."

"He hit you?" I stare at him aghast.

"Now and then. Usually it was just words. Insults. He could be really nasty when he'd had a few."

"What about your sister? Does he hit her too?"

"Wouldn't dare." Jack takes one hand off the steering wheel and rubs his chin. "Not now."

"How do you mean?"

He sighs. Does that hand in his hair thing. "The last time – I mean, the last time he laid into me, over my school report when I was fifteen – I lost it a bit. Hit him back."

Glancing at me, he sees the look on my face. "Not that hard – he was drunk, I didn't need to. It was only to get him to back off. But that was kind of the end of the line for me, you know? I'd had enough. So I left. Told him if he ever laid a finger on Phoebe, I'd kill him, then I walked out and never went back."

I can't speak for a minute. I feel shivery. Shaken. "When was this?"

"About eight years ago. Phoebe was quite little."

"So I guess you don't get to see much of her then?"

He shakes his head. "Now and then. When he's not around."

I exhale slowly, and turn to Jack. "Would you have done it?" I ask quietly. "Killed him, I mean."

Jack looks round at me and laughs. A short, hard bark of a laugh. "You don't think much of me, do you, Chicory?" He drums his fingers on the steering wheel. "Not that I can blame you."

I sit there in silence, watching the scenery flash by. I've run out of questions. I'm feeling drained. As if every last ounce of energy has been sucked out of me. I shut my eyes. Listen to the sounds of the engine, the wheels on the tarmac.

"Tell me about a movie you watched," he says out of the blue.

I open my eyes. He keeps his on the road. I think back to the last thing I saw at the cinema – that stupid romcom, right before Jack almost ran me over in the car park. No, not that.

Then I remember the film Max and I watched that last week he was home, one night while Mum and Dad were out. Max only came down to check the news, but when it started he was glued the whole time, barely speaking until nearly the end.

His face floats before me and I have to swallow before I can speak. "Did you ever see that documentary they made about the French man who crossed between the World Trade Centre buildings on a tightrope?" I try to remember what it's called, but the title escapes me.

"The towers are gone," Jack says, almost irritably.

"Yeah, I know that. It was back in the seventies, long before 9/11."

"Never saw it." Jack glances at me. "Did he make it?"

I nod, remembering how Max leaned forwards, staring intently at the screen as the man set one foot on that impossibly high wire, cautiously testing his weight before taking his first step. Then another. And another. He had one of those long, bendy poles held out in front of him and he swayed slightly as the wind blew between the towers.

It was painful to watch. It seemed to take for ever and you could barely breathe during any of it. But it's not the film I remember, so much as what Max said to me afterwards.

I turn to Jack. "Imagine you were there, back then, in that crowd in New York." I choose my words carefully, keeping my eyes fixed on his face. "Standing there on the ground, looking up between those huge buildings that stretch up into the sky. And right at the top, halfway between the two, you can see this tiny pinprick."

Jack swings his eyes to mine. "Your point being?"

"Just listen. You know it's a man. He's up there, on a tightrope, moving one step at a time, incredibly slowly."

He gives me a longer, more questioning look. "Where exactly are you going with this, Chicory?"

"Imagine, when he's about halfway across, he starts wobbling. Most of the people around you gasp, but one or two begin to cheer. The point is, most people want him to keep his balance, to make it safely to the other side. But some want to see him fall. So what I'm asking you is, which one are you?"

He frowns and clears his throat. "How do you mean?"

"I mean, do you want him to survive, or do you want him to fall? You choose. You don't have to tell me," I say, "but you do have to know. You need to know what kind of person you have in the heart of you."

Jack doesn't say anything, keeping his eyes fixed on the road ahead. He has his lips pressed firmly together and he's not even blinking. I can tell he's thinking it over.

And I have to ask myself again what that face is hiding.

I shut my eyes again. Remember Max watching me as he asked the same question. His searching gaze, like he was trying to peer into the very soul of me.

Though he didn't have to look so hard. He knew which one I'd choose. And all this time I'd assumed Max would make the same choice.

But now I wonder. What kind of person did my brother really have at the heart of him?

We never know, I realize, not about anyone. Not until things go bad. It's only then you discover what people are made of, by the choices they make.

But by then it's often too late.

31

tuesday 13th september

No sign of Jack when I wake, only a mess of blankets on the sofa. I try to check the time on my phone, but still can't get it to turn on, so get out of bed and peek through the curtains. It's light, but barely. All I can make out is a grassy bank surrounding the car park.

A small frisson of relief when I see Jack's car is still over in the corner.

I turn on the motel room TV and find the news. It's in Swedish, but a digital clock at the bottom of the screen tells me it's only ten to seven. I consider going back to sleep for a bit – I still feel exhausted – but decide to use the extra time to get in some practice. If I sing softly, I shouldn't disturb anyone.

I'm limbering up with a few scales when there's a knock on the door. "You decent?" Jack calls out quietly.

"Hang on." I splash water on my face in the bathroom and run my fingers through my hair, then let him in. He barely glances at me.

I go over to the window to draw back the curtains.

"No, leave it." Jack's tone is sharp and my hand shrinks

back. "We need to go." He picks up his rucksack and disappears out the door.

I stuff my things into my bag and follow Jack to the car. He's taking long strides, like he can't get out of here fast enough.

"What's the hurry?" I ask as I do up my seat belt. Jack doesn't answer, just looks behind him, swings the car out in reverse, and accelerates through the exit.

I lapse into silence as we roar up the main road. He seems to have forgotten the speed limit. We're hitting nearly eighty-five and overtaking every other vehicle on the road.

A lorry pulls out suddenly, right in front of us, and Jack has to swerve to avoid it. A blare of horns as we race past.

"Jesus," I gasp.

"Sorry," he mutters, but doesn't slow down. Signs to towns with unpronounceable names whizz by. I stare out the side window at the blur of the landscape – it's less scary than looking ahead. My head feels woozy and my stomach is cramping with lack of food. I'm thirsty too, craving something to remove the stale taste of sleep.

A couple of hours later we pull in at a garage and Jack fills the tank, looking impatient, his eyes fixed on the cars streaming past.

"Want something to eat?" he points towards the Burger King on the other side of the road.

I nod. We drive over to the car park. Three lorries are pulled up opposite. A man eyes me hungrily from one with a Bulgarian plate; Jack glares at him till he turns away.

"Wait here," Jack says, locking the door behind him.

"Water," I call after him. "Not Coke. And just a roll or…"

But he's gone. Five minutes later he returns with a couple of burgers that fill the car with the stink of grease. I get out and sit on grass that's still damp with dew.

"Here." Jack passes me the smaller bag as he bites into his burger.

I shake my head.

"Check it out."

I peer in and pull out a round package. Unwrap it, waiting for the smell of meat to assault me, but it's a veggie burger. I give it a sniff. Not bad, and thankfully it comes with a generous helping of salad. I look back into the paper carrier – there's a small portion of chips and a bottle of Ramlösa mineral water.

I throw Jack an appreciative glance, but he keeps his gaze directed at the entrance to the car park.

"Thanks," I say. This gets his attention. He leans out and offers me a bite of his burger, smirking as I shy my head away.

"Go on," he says. "I reckon you need the protein."

I pull a disgusted face. "I'd rather die."

Jack's expression reverts to something more serious. "Don't say that, Chicory. Ever."

My cheeks flush with shame, and I'm wondering again about this whole "chicory" thing when a loud trilling sound distracts Jack. He pulls his phone out of his pocket and glances at the screen. Hesitates before accepting the call.

"What do you want, Manny?"

I watch Jack's face darken as he listens to the reply. Notice the stubble that's appearing, giving his cheeks a shadowy, more sinister look. He keeps the phone pressed close to his ear. He doesn't speak, but his expression hardens. All at once he punches a button to end the call and opens the passenger door.

"Get in," he barks. "We have to go."

I grab my food and clamber in, and Jack speeds off up the road. The sky comes over gloomy again, grey clouds hanging low, leaving only a small, bright band of light towards the horizon. Jack turns towards Stockholm on the E20.

"Who's Manny?" I ask, once the car is cruising steadily north.

Jack runs his hand over his cheek, leans back in his seat. "Did you know the magnetic field of the Earth has flipped over many times?" he says after a minute or so of silence. Changing the subject.

I don't reply, annoyed he won't tell me what's going on.

"Think about it," he adds. "If you'd stood around here with a compass three-quarters of a million years ago, it would have pointed south."

"Really?" I decide to let the whole Manny thing go for now. Clearly Jack has no intention of telling me who he is.

"Yeah. And they reckon it could start to shift again, any time."

"*Really?*" I repeat, only more sceptical this time. Maybe he's making it up. Who knows if anything Jack says is true?

He looks at me and laughs. "I'm not kidding, Chicory. Check it out on the net if you don't believe me."

I try to imagine it. True south. A world turned upside-down. And it hits me that it's already happened – at least to me. My whole world flipped right over so it's impossible to get my bearings.

"Shit," Jack hisses, under his breath.

I glance at him. "What is it?"

He points at a light flashing on the dashboard. A warning light. He spins to peer out the back window and I follow his gaze. Smoke or steam is billowing out behind us.

Jack thumps the steering wheel, mouth clenched tight, then swings over onto the verge. He jumps out the car and opens the bonnet. Another cloud of steam emerges and Jack backs away.

I get out and stand behind him. "What's going on?"

Jack nods. "I think a gasket has gone."

"Is that bad?"

His grimace passes for an answer. "We're going to have to get it to a garage."

"How?" I glance up and down the road.

Jack shrugs. "I dunno. We'll need somebody to tow us."

"Do you have breakdown cover?"

"Er, no…" His laugh is brittle.

"So what are we going to do?"

"I'll have to walk or hitch to the nearest garage."

I look at him. "I'll come with you."

"No, Sarah, you stay here," Jack says, shaking his head. "Someone has to stay with the car."

I chew the inside of my lip. "How long will you be?"

He shrugs again. "No idea. Depends where the next garage is. And whether they speak English. My Swedish is a little rusty.

"Keep the doors locked," he adds, grabbing his jacket from the car.

I wait till Jack disappears round the bend in the road before starting to search. I check the front glove compartment first, and all the side pockets. Look under the seats and run my hands round the sides of the upholstery. I get out and open the boot and rummage through his bag – only clothes and underwear and a few toiletries.

I kneel on the tarmac and scan under the chassis. All I can see are pipes and bolts and other stuff I can't identify. Nothing seems out of place. I get back up and stalk round the car, even kicking the tyres, vaguely remembering something about drugs smuggled in their inner tubes.

I don't find anything, but I'm not taking much comfort from that. Trouble is I've no idea what I'm looking for, nor how much. And let's face it, there could be a thousand ways to conceal drugs in a car.

I give up. Climb back into the front seat and lock the door and try my phone again. It flickers into life just long enough for me to see the battery is full, before blinking out again.

Damn. I sit there staring at it, and then it occurs to me. I can't even ring for help.

With this comes a crowd of other panicky thoughts. What if someone from that gang really is following us? I think of that man Jack told me about, the one who heads it up. Tommy Crace. What does he look like? I wonder.

And what if he's watching me now?

Oh god. The moment it crosses my mind the hairs stand up on the back of my neck and I start to sweat, even though it's getting pretty cold with the heating off. I watch each car whizzing past me, half expecting them to suddenly stop and pull over.

What would I do if one did? I'm really frightened now, my pulse beginning to climb. Jesus. I should have asked Jack for his phone.

How long has he been gone? I've lost track of time, and I can't turn on the ignition and see the clock on the dashboard because he's taken the keys.

I sit back in the seat, close my eyes and try to breathe evenly. Remember my singing exercises. Long steady inhale, then breathe out, counting slowly in my head till I get to twenty. Over and over again.

But I keep seeing Mrs Perry's face as I do it, and that makes me feel worse. As if she exists in a world a million miles away from here. A nice, safe, normal world where you don't take off abroad with a convicted drug dealer and find yourself abandoned in the middle of nowhere.

I'm so tired that somehow I doze off, despite my uneasiness. I wake to the sound of a car pulling up. My eyes snap open. A red four-wheel drive has stopped right opposite me, on the other side of the carriageway. My heart starts to race again, as fast as my thoughts.

What should I do? Try to hide? Get out and run? Flag down a car for help?

Jack said to stay in the car. I sink low in my seat, hoping it looks empty. But I catch sight of someone already opening the door to the SUV and getting out.

Oh god.

Seconds later a thump on the window, I look up, terrified.

It's Jack. He turns away, waving at the driver of the red car; it pulls back into the road and disappears.

Jack opens the driver's door and jumps in. "Good news or the bad?" he asks.

"Good," I say, sitting up straight, trying to make out like I haven't been blindly panicking.

"There's a garage about fifteen miles up the road."

"Okay. So what's the bad news?"

"They can't come and get us till tomorrow morning. The tow truck's picking up someone a few hours away and won't be back until later tonight. The bloke at the garage says we could get a rescue service to come out from Vad-somewhere-or-other, but it'll cost us."

"How much?"

"More than I've got, Chicory. I need to save some cash for the repair."

Another lurch of guilt. I should have thought of this. I should have brought more money with me. It was all such a rush, leaving, I didn't have time to think everything through.

"Can't we put it on a credit card? I'll pay you back."

Jack raises an eyebrow. "Do I strike you as the kind of person who comes with a good credit rating?"

I think about how much I've got in my bag. Not a lot. Certainly not enough for a motel room.

"So where are we going to sleep?" I ask. The light is already beginning to fade and the air is growing colder by the minute.

"In here," says Jack, with a grim smile. "You can have the back, if you like."

32

wednesday 14th september

I don't get much sleep. It's not only that the back seat is seriously uncomfortable, even if I can lie on my side in a cramped fetal position. Or the fact that it's freezing and I've only my coat to cover me. But more because I spend half the night worrying about whether I'll make it home in time for my audition.

Or even make it home at all.

I run through my options. All two of them. Hitchhike to the nearest station and get the next train south. But I'm not sure I've got enough money for a ticket, and I'd have to ring Mum or Dad to get them to pay for it. And if I do that, I know I'll have to tell them what on earth I'm doing out here.

Or option two. Carry on and pray I don't miss the ferry home.

Somehow this feels the only real choice I've got. I have to sort this out once and for all.

I feel a rush of anger towards Max. The trouble he's inflicted on our family. The danger he's brought to our door. Why did he do it, if it wasn't for the money? Why didn't he consider the consequences of making that bloody stuff?

I think back to how my brother used to tease me, calling me "brainbox" and "Mensa child" whenever we got into an argument. Like I was really dumb.

But what's the point of being clever if you dump everyone in a mess like this? I ask myself. If you can't see when something makes no kind of sense at all?

I feel a good ten years older by the time the tow truck pulls up a couple of hours after it gets light. It takes five minutes to hitch up the car, then Jack and I squeeze into the small cab with the garage man. Aside from a brief nod hello, he doesn't speak the whole way. I'm guessing his English isn't so great.

Not that I'm in the mood for conversation. All I can focus on is finding somewhere to go to the loo and clean my teeth. As soon as we get to the garage, I grab my bag and bolt into the little room with a ladies' sign while Jack disappears into the workshop.

He's waiting by the office when I come out. "It's the head gasket. They have to go into town to get a part, but they reckon they can have it ready by mid-afternoon."

I do a quick mental calculation. We should be at the summer house by this evening. If I can find what I need and we leave straight away, I might be okay.

Just.

*　　*　　*

The landscape is changing now, open fields replaced by endless stretches of pine and birch forest, dark and forbidding as you glimpse into their depths. Miles and miles of it, only the odd dead stump sticking high above the saplings like a telegraph pole.

Up ahead somebody has sprayed graffiti on a rocky outcrop by the road. Great big rounded letters, their zany neon colours in bold contrast to the light grey stone.

"Jeez," mutters Jack.

"What?" I ask, surprised he's even noticed. His eyes rarely waver from the road ahead, or his rear-view mirror.

"Bloody Volvos. I wouldn't be seen dead driving one. Even if they are more reliable than this pile of crap."

I study the traffic for the next few miles. He's right. Every other car is a Volvo.

I remember the one we had for years, and the times Max and I rode in the back, down to France or Italy, once all the way to Spain. The endless hours bickering and needling and goading each other with surreptitious pinches and slaps, kept just below Mum's radar as she studied the map in the front. No satnav back then.

Inevitably one of us would go too far and Dad would shout, and we'd revert to smirking and pulling faces, allies again.

A wave of sadness washes over me as I realize how happy we were then. Not that we knew it at the time.

When it happens I'm so lost in my thoughts I barely notice. Jack yanks on the steering wheel and we spin into a U-turn, heading back up the road the way we came. I peer into my side mirror. Right behind us a large black car does the same manoeuvre.

My blood goes cold. Oh god…oh shit…*it's true*. They're really after us.

Jack races down the carriageway. I watch the needle of the speedometer steadily climbing…sixty…seventy… eighty…

"Jack…"

"Not now!"

Suddenly we veer off into a side road, accelerating along a narrow lane through the forest, pine trees whizzing by perilously close. Jack turns sharp left and we bounce over a mud track. Things tumble around the car, and I grab the handle above my door to keep my balance.

"Hold on!"

Jack hauls on the steering wheel again and all at once we're in among the trees. The suspension groans as we hit a small rock and he swerves to avoid a stump. We come to a halt in a mass of moss and ferns.

"Stay here!" Jack barks, leaning over and sliding an arm under his seat. He's fiddling with something, like it's stuck.

"Damn!" He twists himself round so he can reach even further. There's a faint ripping sound, and his hand emerges holding a fat brown envelope with duct tape hanging from each side.

What the…? I don't even get to finish the thought before he rips it open and my breath freezes in my throat as I glimpse cold grey metal.

Not drugs he was hiding. Not drugs at all.

A gun.

Jack has got a gun.

I yelp in shock. But before I can say anything, do anything, think anything, he's out the car and running through the trees.

I sit there, whimpering, my breathing jagged with fear and dread. I sit there and it's like time is suspended. No time at all and all the time in the world passes before I hear the shot.

And the silence that follows.

I keep perfectly still, too frightened to move or scream or cry, and wait for whatever will happen to happen. Until it feels as if that's all I've ever been doing, just sitting here, waiting for it all to end.

wednesday 14th september

He's lying in the grass by the other car. Slumped face forward, near the wheel, as if he'd tried to make a run for it. Tears spring to my eyes and I clamp my hands over my mouth to suppress a scream.

"No!" My voice comes out as a choking sound. Almost a wail. "Stop!"

But Jack doesn't stop. He reverses past, his face wearing the same mask of grim determination it had when he jumped back in the driving seat and fired the engine to life.

"Jack, stop!" I scream again, as he keeps backing the car in the direction we came, our tyres bumping over rocks and tree roots. I stare at the body on the ground, until we're enveloped by trees and it disappears.

Suddenly I can't breathe. I reach for the door handle and throw it open and the brakes screech as Jack slams his foot down hard. I fall out of the car, running and stumbling back through the trees.

"Sarah, for Christ's sake…"

I ignore him. I'm sprinting now, branches of fir

whipping my face as I push my way through. Then a sharp, fierce pain in my chest brings me to a halt. I bend over and throw up into a pile of mossy rocks lying at my feet. I heave until there is nothing left to bring up.

But I still can't get any air into my lungs. My breathing has dwindled to short, faltering gasps, interspersed with sobs.

A hand seizes me by the shoulder. "For god's sake, Sarah…"

I hit him. Swing my right fist round as hard as I can and punch him in the jaw. Pain shoots up through my fingers, a hot flare of agony that makes me cry out.

Jack's head snaps back. He clutches his face and looks at me in shock.

"Christ, Chicory, you pack one hell of a—"

I swing at him again. This time he steps back neatly and grabs my wrist with one hand, the other coming up to grasp my left arm.

"Pack it in," he hisses. He holds my wrists firm as I struggle. "Get a bloody grip!"

"*You killed him!*" All at once I find my voice. "You *killed* him, Jack!" I glare at him wildly, wondering if this is the first time he's done it. Or the last.

Jesus… Maybe I'm next.

Jack looks at me and twitches his jaw. "No, he's not dead. He's…he's just taking some time out."

I glare at him.

"Listen to me, Sarah. He's not dead. I promise you."

"But I heard it. *I heard the shot*…I saw you take the gun…"

I start crying again and he grips my arms and shakes me hard before pulling me forwards, bringing my face so close to his I can feel his breath on my skin as he speaks.

"I didn't shoot him, okay? I knocked him out, then I shot his tyre. So they couldn't follow us."

"They?" I stare at him, eyes mad with fear and my stomach iced in dread.

Jack releases me and runs both hands through his hair as he glances through the trees. "Yes, Sarah. *They*. There'll be another one around here somewhere."

"How did you manage…?" I can't actually say it.

"I got lucky," he says, rubbing his chin. "He didn't see me coming." He looks round us again. "But let's not push our luck. We have to get out of here. Fast."

He pulls something from his jeans. The gun. Swiftly he removes the bullets and lobs it into the forest.

I watch, bewildered. "But won't we need—?"

"It's not mine," he barks. "Mine's here." He opens his jacket so I can see the handle sticking out of the inside pocket, then turns and strides back towards the car. I stand there. Hesitating. Is he telling the truth? How do I know whether to believe him?

And that man. Shouldn't we go back and check he's all right?

Don't be ridiculous, says a clear voice in my head. And suddenly I'm running. Running back to the car.

I jump in beside Jack and we speed away.

*   *   *

We sit in silence for maybe twenty miles. I'm shaking as I stare out the window, neck craned to the side so I can't see Jack, not even out of the corner of my eye.

"Sarah." His voice heavy and stern. "Listen to me. I know you think I'm bad, and I am bad, it's true. But I'm not *that* bad, okay?"

I bite my lip. Lizzie's words ring in my ears. *He's bad news... Stay away from him.*

"Do you hear me, Sarah? I didn't kill him, though it would probably have been better for us if I had. He's not dead. I just gave him a bang on the head. I had to."

"Who was it?" I ask. "Tommy Crace?"

Jack shakes his head. "One of his sidekicks, Evan."

I close my eyes, but he grips my face with his left hand and forces me to look at him. "You still don't trust me, do you?"

I blink.

"Do you?" he says, almost aggressively. Accusingly. "I come with you, all this way, and you still don't trust me."

A tear rolls down my cheek and I wipe it away fiercely with the heel of my hand. "What choice do I have?"

Jack thumps his fist against the top of the dashboard then lapses back into silence. Neither of us speaks for ten minutes as we carry on hurtling north.

"We should go home," he says suddenly. "They know where we're going. They've got it all worked out."

I turn my head and he looks towards me. "Are you listening? We should go back. It's too risky."

"And then what?" My voice sounds croaky and ridiculously quiet, like a child.

Jack raises his hand and rubs his forehead, the other gripping the steering wheel so tight his knuckles are turning white.

"I don't know. I'll talk to them. I'll sort something out. But we can't go there, Sarah, they'll find us."

"But you stopped them," I say.

Jack sighs. "Not for long, Chicory. Not for long."

I stare back out the window, squeezing my eyes shut. My hand goes up to the amethyst I'm still wearing around my neck, the gift from Mum and Dad. I twist it in my fingers and come to a decision. I won't run. I won't spend the rest of my life feeling this afraid.

I'm going to see this through to the end.

"No." I open my eyes and fix them on the road ahead, my voice louder and clearer now. "No, we're not turning back. We're going on."

34

wednesday 14th september

It's nearly dark and we're lost. I thought I remembered the way, but now it comes to it, I find I haven't a clue.

I peer again at the little map we bought in the garage ten miles back, trying to work out where to go. Turn left off the main road, then take the next right through the village and follow the lane down towards the lake. I remember a dirt track that ran parallel to the water for a mile or so, before branching off at a farm. I'm pretty sure Gran's summer house is over on the left, through a copse of birch trees.

But somewhere we must have gone wrong, and now we're lost amongst the endless pines. Even the satnav is defeated, its little yellow arrow meandering around in an off-road oblivion.

"Do you recognize anything yet?"

I glance at Jack. He looks edgy and alert despite the lack of sleep, still regularly checking his mirror. I can feel irritation radiating off him like heat.

I chew my bottom lip and gaze ahead, willing myself to see some kind of landmark. Anything. But it's just mile after mile after mile of forest, with barely any other cars on the road now – not even a Volvo. And all these country lanes look the same, flanked with trees and boulders and the occasional house.

"Trees, rock, sky," mutters Jack, his voice full of bitterness and fatigue.

I'm close to tears as he stops and turns around, heading in the direction we came. "Let's go back to town and give it another try from there."

I nod.

It's barely past seven but already the light is dwindling. I wonder if we could find a cheap hotel, or whether we'll end up sleeping in the car again. I wipe my eyes. I'm so tired. I just want to be at home, tucked up in my own bed. Far away from all this.

Jack was right. This whole trip was a bad idea. A really bad idea.

But there's no going back now.

"There!"

I point to a small track turning off the road. Right beside it is one of those metal mailboxes with a couple of name tags underneath and a painting of a red cockerel on the side.

"This way! I remember this!" I nod at the mailbox. I was looking the other way before and must have missed it.

"You sure?" Jack slows to a halt, eyeing the track dubiously.

"I think so," I say. Praying I'm right.

"Okay."

He pulls on the steering wheel and bumps the car down the track. Within minutes we're passing the neighbouring farm and idling along the left-hand fork.

A few seconds later I spot the summer house, a glimpse of dark crimson between the trees. I point it out to Jack, but he drives right past.

"Where are you going?" I ask, bewildered.

Jack doesn't reply, only carries on another hundred yards until the track runs out, then turns into the trees and parks the car as deep into the woods as he can get.

Hiding it, I realize, with a jolt of fear.

He kills the ignition and we sit there for a while, the engine ticking and grumbling as it starts to cool. Hard to believe it was so warm when we left home; here the evening air is taking on an icy chill even though it's barely autumn.

"You got a key?" asks Jack.

I shake my head. "It's not usually locked. But anyhow, I know where the spare is kept."

We grab our bags out the boot and walk up to the house. It's exactly as I remember – a plain red box with a large raised porch and windows either side of the door. A single chimney for the wood stove. I push open the gate to the picket fence surrounding the garden, though now there's only grass inside, along with a few cherry and apple trees.

"Who looks after this place?" Jack asks.

"The farmer up the road. He rents it out occasionally and keeps the income."

I climb the steps onto the wooden porch and turn the door handle. Locked.

I bend over and fumble around the door frame in the twilight, searching for the key. Nothing. Shit.

I walk right round the house, checking all the obvious places someone might hide it, while Jack glances nervously around us. "We have to get in fast."

"The farmer will have a key. I'll go and fetch it."

"No!" he snaps.

I look at him in surprise.

"It's better no one knows we're here."

"But he wouldn't tell any—"

"Better for him too."

I swallow. "Okay. So…any ideas?"

Jack stalks around the house again, sizing up the windows.

"I suppose we could try to smash one," I say reluctantly. "But it wouldn't be easy. They're triple-glazed."

He shakes his head. "Too noisy."

Returning to the front door, he examines the lock. It's a Yale one that takes a small, flat key.

Jack pulls his wallet out of his pocket and removes a plastic card, the kind you get from shops for collecting loyalty points. Holding down the handle, he slides it in the gap between the lock and the door. He wiggles it, keeping the pressure on the handle, then bends the card back hard towards the middle of the door. I'm thinking it's about to snap in two when there's a faint click and the door swings open.

"What the hell...?" I gasp. He made it look so simple. *Like he's had some practice,* says a voice in my head.

Jack smiles as if he heard. "Yeah, Chicory. Easy once you know how."

35

wednesday 14th september

The summer house has a damp, musty smell, like no one has been in here for years, not just a few months.

I walk into the living room and dump my bag on the floor. Reach out to switch on the light, praying the electricity has been left on.

"Don't!" Jack almost shouts. I snatch back my hand as if stung.

My eyes slowly adjust to the dimness. The place looks so empty. A pair of old high-back armchairs round the little coffee table, two wooden benches and a dining table taking up the rest of the space in the living area.

I peer into the bathroom downstairs. The reek of damp is stronger in here and I notice a small pool of water near the shower. Something must be leaking. In the kitchen, however, everything seems okay. There's nothing on any of the work surfaces, only a large aluminium kettle sitting on the stove. I walk over and turn on the tap; water gushes out, ice cold to the touch.

Moving back into the hallway, I stand at the bottom of the stairs, gazing up into the gloom. Hesitating, though

I know I have to face it.

This is something I can't put off any longer.

I climb up to the landing, glancing in the double bedroom at the empty bed before turning round. The door to the smaller room is shut. I hover there for a moment, then force myself to walk over and twist the handle. A small groan from the hinges and I step inside.

Both the mattresses are bare, apart from a couple of pillows stacked upright against each headboard. The curtains are open and there's nothing in the tiny room except the two single beds either side of a pine chest of drawers.

I take another step in, my legs trembling. *Which one did Max…?* I can't finish the thought. I don't want to go there, though now I'm standing here in the room in which he died, I realize this is why I had to come.

Max. *Oh god.*

An image of my brother and me sleeping in here, under those old flowery eiderdowns that smelled of dust and cut grass. I close my eyes and give a little whelp of pain. Grief floods through me, washing my breath away, leaving me shaking and sobbing. A fierce ache in my heart sweeps all my fear aside as I yearn for his presence. Find only his absence.

Max. I'll never see his face, hear his voice again. It's unbelievable. Unimaginable.

Unbearable.

I sink onto the mattress of the nearest bed and bury

my face into the scratchy feather pillow and let out a long, low wail.

Seconds later I feel a hand on my head. Sense Jack kneeling on the floor beside me, caressing my hair. He doesn't speak, simply keeps up the rhythmic stroking and slowly, eventually, my breathing slows to normal and the choking sobs subside.

I sit up, wiping my face with the back of my hand. Realize I'm shivering. I can barely make out Jack's features in the darkness.

He stands and goes out into the hallway. I hear him open the door to the airing cupboard and he returns with a blanket and an old bedspread. Leaning over, he pulls the boots off my feet and I sink back onto the bed.

It's too early to sleep, I think, as he drapes the blanket over me, but barely has the thought taken root than I'm sinking down into oblivion.

In my dream I'm fleeing from something. Something so nameless and dreadful that my mind refuses to give it shape. I'm with Max. He's running beside me and we're moments away from making it to safety when he stumbles and falls.

"Go on, Sarah," his voice cries out after me. "Don't look back."

But I stop. I can't leave my brother behind. Can't leave him here all alone.

I look back. But he's gone and I cry out and wake from the dream with a gasp, my heart racing, Max's voice still echoing in my head. I'm sweating beneath the blankets, though the air around me is sharp and cold. The room is completely dark. For a few seconds I have no clue where I am.

Then I remember, and turn towards the window. The curtains must be closed because I can't see anything. No moon, no stars. I lie there, waiting for my heart rate to diminish and my dream to die away, ears alert for any sound.

Jack must be in the next room, sleeping in my parents' bed. I consider getting up to find him, but my limbs feel huge and heavy, as if bits of me are still asleep.

I lay my head back on the pillow, willing myself to drift off again. Then I hear it. A noise like a large twig snapping. Near the house.

I sit up with a start, listening, my heart revving up again like an engine thrust straight into top gear. Hard to make out anything above its insistent thump.

But there it is again. Louder this time. More of a definite crack.

"Jack?" My voice emerges small and shaky.

"Shhhh…" I hear him moving across the hallway to the stairs, almost soundlessly, as if he's sliding in his socks. A slight creak as he sets his weight on the first stair.

He makes his way down step by slow step. I slip out of bed, fully awake now, feeling my way towards the door.

"Stay there," Jack hisses.

Another creak as he edges down the wooden staircase. I can't see him, but somehow I know he has that gun in his hand.

I should be horrified, I think. I should be pleading with him to drop it.

But all I feel is thankful.

Again a noise, this time a cross between a grunt and a protracted screech. I jump in alarm, my heart in my mouth.

And then I understand.

"Jack," I call out softly. "Jack, it's okay. Come here."

Jack bounds up the stairs and joins me by the window. I've pulled back the curtains and the faintest light shines from the moon, framed by clouds, illuminating the lawn and trees below.

Then we see it. Ambling back towards the open gate, huge and dark, its great antlers suspended over its long, pendulous face.

An elk.

"Jesus," exhales Jack, relief in his voice.

"Probably foraging for food. They come in after the apples. They eat them when they've fallen off the tree and fermented. It makes them tipsy."

"Nearly gave me a bloody heart attack." He watches the elk as it lumbers away into the darkness.

"Could be worse. Could have been a wolf."

"Wolf?" asks Jack. "Seriously?"

"Seriously," I echo. "There's quite a few in Sweden." I'm smiling, though he can't see. "So you'd better watch out."

"Sure," he says in a nonchalant voice, but I sense him shiver beside me in the darkness.

36

thursday 15th september

I oversleep, exhausted from the journey. By the time I surface and go downstairs, it's nearly midday. Jack is sitting in the armchair, studying the map we bought yesterday in the garage.

"You should have woken me," I say.

He shrugs. "I thought you could do with the sleep." He points to a large area of blue in the centre of the map. "It's pretty big, isn't it?"

"The lake?"

"More like a small sea, I'd say."

I nod. "Yeah. It stretches all the way over to Östersund. About five miles across at the widest point."

Last time we were here Dad borrowed an outboard motor for the boat and we chugged right round the coastline; it took us the best part of a day. Max caught two large fish, and Dad wanted to cook them for supper, but my brother wasn't having any of it.

Live and let live, he said, and let them go.

I glance around the kitchen. My stomach aches and my head is throbbing. I get a glass and run some water out the tap, downing it in several gulps.

"Here." Jack reaches into his bag, pulling out a muesli bar and holding it out to me.

I pull a face.

"Beggars can't be choosers." He chucks it on the coffee table and returns his attention to the map. I retrieve the muesli bar and chew in silence. The sticky sweetness is overpowering, but by the time I finish I'm feeling slightly better. Then I head for the stairs.

"Okay, so what do you want to do?" Jack folds the map and sits back.

"Nothing," I say. "Leave it to me."

He shrugs and looks out the window. I start up in the bedroom. It doesn't take long. There's not many places Max could have hidden anything. I check in the pine chest, lifting out each drawer to see if he might have taped anything underneath. I pull up the old cotton rug from the floorboards. I run my hand around the back of the curtains. Zilch.

I repeat the same exercise in my parents' bedroom, searching every inch of the large white wardrobe. I try to pull it away from the wall, but it's too heavy for me to shift.

"Here, let me help."

I turn to see Jack standing in the doorway. He comes over and drags the wardrobe into the centre of the room. Nothing behind it except a couple of old cobwebs and a few dead flies.

He heaves it back into place and gazes around, then lies

on the floorboards and sticks his head under the bed, running his hands between the wooden slats and the mattress.

I wonder if he's guessed what I'm looking for.

We move into the bathroom. I rifle through the cupboards while Jack checks in the cistern, then pulls the plastic panel off the bath and feels around the gap between the tub and the floor.

Downstairs I go through everything. Take the mugs and plates out the kitchen cupboard, even check in the cooking pots and pans and those old casserole dishes Gran used to collect. Jack finds a torch and shines the beam into the space underneath the oven and the fridge. We tip back all the furniture in the living room, prising off the fabric that lines the underside of the armchairs so I can slip my hand inside.

It takes half the afternoon to scour the whole house. By the time we've finished I'm almost fizzing with frustration. Maybe I'm wrong, I think. Maybe he didn't hide them at all. Perhaps Max tore out those pages and destroyed them.

But he wouldn't. I'm not sure how I know that, but I do. I don't believe Max could have made himself do it.

I glance at Jack. He must have worked this all out. Not once has he asked what we're hunting for, insisting on covering the outside of the house himself in case we were seen. It gives me an uneasy feeling, like a nagging toothache I'm hoping will subside without having to pay it more attention.

I make a mug of black tea with some tea bags I found in the back of the cupboard and stand by the living-room window, staring out across the lake. There's a slight haziness over the water, the hint of mist.

I think of our last visit, how Max and I took the rowing boat out for hours every day, drifting around with his fishing rod stuck over the back. Apart from that trip with Dad, we never caught much, but neither of us cared. It was great just being out there, on our own, with the sky and the water and the wild little islands that only the gulls inhabit.

Something inside me contracts at the memory and I get a strong urge to simply get in the car and drive away. I was mad to come here. Insane.

Everywhere I look I feel the weight of memories. The cherry tree where Max broke his toe climbing after fruit. The tall pine up near the farm where I spotted an osprey's nest. The island just across the water – I smile remembering the first time Max and I camped there alone, spending half the night awake, terrified by the sounds of the natural world around us, neither of us willing to admit we wanted to go home.

The island.

I gaze out over the lake again. You can't see it from the house, hidden by birch trees and the curve of the bay. But I know it's there, only a ten-minute row away.

"I'm going out." I grab my coat and pull on my boots.

"Where?" Jack's head jerks up.

"Just out."

"I'll come with you."

I turn round, mouth open to protest, but Jack is already up and approaching the door.

"I'm not letting you out of my sight," he says in a tone I now know better than to argue with.

But why? asks that voice in my head as we emerge outside. *Why does he want to come? To keep an eye on me, make sure I'm okay?*

Or to be certain he's there if I actually find anything?

I shake the thought away and go round the back of the house, peering into the crawl space underneath. The oars are still there. I pick one up and hand it to Jack, take the other myself. We wedge the front door ajar with a stone, then I lead the way down the footpath towards the lake.

As we round the corner I see the little glade of silver birch, their white trunks near luminous in the autumn light. To the right, the small pavilion overlooking the wooden jetty. To the left, veiled by the trees, a small natural harbour in amongst the reeds.

There are two boats. The one belonging to the farmer lies overturned on dry land, covered with a tarpaulin. Ours is floating in the shallows, tethered with a long rope. It's full of twigs and leaves and greenish-black water, looking as if it hasn't been used in years.

Jack and I drag the boat out and heave it over, letting the dirty water drain for a minute before righting it and pushing it back into the lake. I'm praying it doesn't leak as I climb inside and fix the oars into the rowlocks. Jack gives the boat a shove, then jumps in, cursing as water seeps into his boots. We drift out through the reeds for a few metres, then I turn the boat and start rowing into the open lake.

As soon as we round the wooded peninsula protecting the harbour, the wind gets up, whipping the surface of the lake into little peaks and valleys. I line up the prow of the boat with the island and heave on the oars, concentrating on cutting them cleanly into the water and propelling the boat forwards.

Within minutes, however, my arms are aching and we're not making much headway. I rest for a moment, letting the boat slowly drift with the current, and see Jack eyeing me with an amused expression.

"Want a hand, Chicory?"

I nod, reluctantly, and shuffle to the end of the boat. Jack takes my seat and picks up the oars. He grips them tightly then drops them into the water, pulling towards him. But the left oar skims the surface without cutting in, pitching the boat to one side.

"Damn," he mutters under his breath, and I realize he's never done this before.

"Lower them in together," I say. "Don't pull until you feel them bite."

He straightens the boat with the right oar, then tries again. This time we lunge forwards and within a minute Jack has the hang of it, rowing with strong, regular movements. We're speeding towards the island, cold spray flying around our faces as the boat skids through the little waves.

I lean over the side, staring into the black depths of the lake. It looks so unfathomably deep. Anything could be living down there. Dark, ugly, nameless things. My insides shudder at the thought.

All at once the sun emerges between the clouds and ignites the surface of the water. I lift my head and watch the sunlight glinting on the tips of the waves like millions of tiny jewels.

It's midweek and there's no one around. We're alone in this vast landscape, so wide and open and wild and lovely, the soothing, rhythmic slap of water against the side of the boat the perfect accompaniment to all this beauty. For a moment I can almost forget why we're here.

But Jack's voice reels me in again. "How much further?" he asks, rowing with his back to the island.

"Another few minutes."

I examine it as we get closer, a large raft of rock looming out of the lake like the fossil of something huge and primal. The right edge smooth and undulating, forming a beach facing the mainland. Beyond, pine and birch cover the remaining ground, from a distance giving the island the appearance of a giant green dome. Though I can see the birch trees are already losing their leaves.

"Steer over to your left," I tell Jack as we close in, pointing towards the small, rocky outcrop that provides a natural harbour near the beach. But Jack shakes his head and rows round to the other side, guiding the boat into the reeds.

So we can't be seen from the mainland.

I jump out onto a rock, leaving Jack to tie up the boat, and walk to the highest part of the island, surveying all the bits I know so well. The long ridge that runs along the centre like a fault line. The small grassy plain down among the birches, perfect for camping. The great slab of granite near the north end, split into three pieces as if stamped on by some ancient Norse god.

From one edge to the other the whole place is no larger than a football field, too small for anyone living around here to bother with. But Max loved this island more than anywhere in the world.

His little Eden, he called it. His paradise.

All at once I sense my brother's presence everywhere around me – in the rocks and trees, in the sound of the water lapping on the rock, the breeze that whips my face. I stand motionless, taking it all in, and the pain in my heart grows so huge I feel I'll shatter from the force of it, and the wind will scatter me across the lake in a thousand little pieces.

I take a deep breath, wiping my cheeks, and glance around for Jack. He's lurking in the wooded area at the back of the island, looking out over the water, half hidden by the trees. Standing guard, I realize, with a surge of fear that snaps me back to our predicament.

Focus, I tell myself, and start exploring the island. I study the rocks, splashed with blotches of bright mustard and pale green lichens, and search in clefts packed with grass and moss. I look down by the fallen pine, its great arc of tree root picked clean now by rain and wind. Make my way round to the grove where tiny yellow flowers bloom in summer, hunting for somewhere that would make a natural hiding place.

I find nothing but an old crisp packet and a tangled length of fishing line and feel a wave of despair. It could be anywhere. Absolutely anywhere.

If it's here at all.

Out in the distance I hear the faint hum of an outboard motor. I peer across the water, standing there for a couple of minutes, watching. But I can't see anything and the noise dies away. A fisherman further up the lake, I guess, getting in a few hours while the weather is good.

I walk over to the promontory that looks out towards the pavilion on the shore, forcing myself to think. *Where, Max?* I ask into the wind. *Where would you put it?*

Nowhere, the sensible part of my brain tells me. I'm wasting my time. Whatever propelled me here, it was never my brother's intention that I came.

Or was it? A memory stirs like a leaf in the breeze. That granite pebble, the one I found on my bedroom floor after the burglary. The one I threw at Max and he brought home with him. His memento of our fight, and this place he loved so much.

I never worked out why it was in my bedroom. Certainly I didn't remove it from Max's desk, and I can't think why Mum or Dad would.

Max did, I realize with a rush of certainty. My brother placed it in my bedroom, on a shelf probably – or maybe in my drawer. Only I didn't notice, not until my room was ransacked and the pebble ended up on the floor.

Max put it there because he wanted to tell me something too important to risk putting into words. That he was coming to the island. Or that he'd left something in this place.

What I'm looking for is here, somewhere. I'm certain now. I just have to find it.

I spin round, trying to put myself in my brother's head. If I had something to hide, something small, where would I put it?

Then I remember.

I check around for Jack. No sign of him. He must still be keeping a lookout on the other side of the island.

I run across the thick tussocks of grass on the central ridge, climbing down to where the granite drops off in a miniature cliff, and duck round the fir tree growing next to it. Squatting on my heels, I inspect the sheer face of the rock in front of me.

Where is it? I'm sure it's here somewhere.

I use my fingers to trace the network of cracks, looking for the glint of metal. One summer Max and I hid coins in these crevices, promising to check they were still there every time we returned. Two five-krona pieces, big silver coins like pirate treasure.

I scratch off the moss with a piece of stick. Sure enough, a glint of metal shines from one of the cracks. I try to pull it out with my fingertips, but it's wedged fast.

Come on, Sarah. *Think*. It's got to be here. I scrape more moss away and trace my thumbnail along the edge of the coin, following the gap in the rock downwards. Near the ground, half concealed by the tree trunk, it widens into a small fissure, about the width of two piano keys.

I inhale deeply and slide in my hand, sideways on, but can't feel anything except cold, damp rock. I force my fingers forwards with a quiver of fear about getting them stuck, then touch something pliable. I push in further, gripping it between my middle and index fingers, pulling gently towards me. I lose my grasp and scrape the back of my knuckles on a sharp piece of stone.

I try again, edging the tips of my fingers further in, and pincer the plastic between them as hard as I can. Then pull back slowly and steadily. Gradually the package emerges from its narrow cave. A thick blue see-through bag, the kind you use to wrap sandwiches, sealed with tape. And inside, clearly visible, several sheets of folded notepaper.

Max's notes. His own island treasure.

I rip open the plastic and unfold the paper. On top, a note scribbled in Max's handwriting.

If you ever find this, Sarah, then you know, and you need these pages. I hope they help. And I'm sorry. Please, somehow, forgive me. Max.

A lump in my throat so big I feel I'm choking. I blink back tears and skim the pages underneath. Numbers and equations I can't even begin to comprehend. But I grasp enough to know that this is what they're after.

The formula.

And I understand, too, why Max chose not to destroy it. He knew these people would stop at nothing. That as a last resort, the only chance to keep us all safe would be to give them what they want.

No matter what the cost.

A sharp snap of a twig underfoot. I look up and that's when I see him. Silhouetted against the pale sunlight, staring down at me and the notes in my hand. His face is partly concealed by shadow, but I can still make out his expression.

My whole body starts to tremble.

37

"Give it to me, Sarah."

I stare at Jack. He's stretching out his arm towards me.

But not offering to help me up.

"Come on." His tone hard, terse.

I swallow. My eyes are beginning to sting. I don't move. I can't.

"Sarah, for Christ's sake, hand it over. We haven't got much time."

He wiggles his fingers at the parcel in my hand. I look at his face. See the determination there and know I've no choice but to do what he says. I give the package to him and he shoves it into his pocket.

What will he do now? I wonder. Leave me here?

Shoot me?

He spins around, eyes roaming the horizon, then looks back down at me.

"You're going to have to make a run for it. Try and get to the boat."

"What?" My voice comes out shaky.

"They'll be here any second."

I gaze at him, wild-eyed.

"Who?"

But the instant I ask, I know. Tommy, Manny, whoever. They've followed us here. To the island.

I've led them right to what they're after. And all at once I realize I've changed my mind. I don't want them to have it at all. Not even Jack.

This stuff has destroyed two lives already. I won't let it ruin any more.

I glance back up at Jack and he extends his hand again.

"Can't we hide?" I ask unsteadily. "Wait till they go?"

Jack shakes his head. "They've seen the boat. They know we're here."

I lift my hand and he hauls me to my feet. We hurry down to the water, but it's too late. Already I can see a motorboat speeding towards us, its roar suddenly subsiding as the man cuts the engine and lets it glide up to the beach.

"Get back into the trees!" Jack hisses, as he crouches behind a large rock.

I run towards the copse at the far end of the island, stumbling over stones and roots, my heart pounding so hard it's difficult to breathe. I squat in a hollow made by a fallen tree.

I can just see Jack hunched behind the rock. He's resting his arm on top, pointing it in the direction of the approaching boat. "Stop right there!" he shouts to the man at the steering wheel.

A sharp ping as something hits the stone. Jack swears and ducks.

Shit. They must have another gun.

A second shot. This time the man on board dives behind the windshield. Jack stands and walks towards the lake, the gun trained on the boat a few metres away.

"Drop it!" Jack yells as he starts to wade into the water. I hear a sharp clatter as something heavy drops onto the deck. The man rises slowly, hands held up to show they're empty. Jack takes another step towards him.

It's then I feel the arm close around my throat.

38

thursday 15th september

He's edging me forwards, shoving me, at the same time gripping my neck so tight I'm struggling to breathe. And there, again, that stringent smell of aftershave, dense and cloying in this clean, fresh air.

Him. The man who mugged me.

All of a sudden, he stumbles on a rock and for a few seconds the pressure on my throat slackens.

"Jack!" I scream, as loudly as I can.

Over by the shore I see Jack look up. I'm pulled to my feet, exposing us both, and I realize this is a trap. The boat driver must have dropped this man off on the island before cruising round to the other side.

They planned it. And it looks as if their scheme is working perfectly. Jack turns towards us, but keeps his gun aimed at the boat.

I feel myself released and shoved forwards. I can't see him, but I'm guessing my captor is armed.

Jesus, part of my mind thinks, *this can't be real. This can't actually be happening.*

"Walk!" a deep voice growls behind me, and I stagger

forwards. I turn and catch a glimpse of a heavy, jowly face before he grabs me roughly and steers me towards the shore, towards a large slab of rock that shelves directly into the water.

Jack's eyes follow our approach, but he doesn't lower his arm.

I get to the end and stop. There's nowhere else to go – except into the lake. I look across at Jack, notice the tension in his jaw.

"Where is it?" the man behind me shouts towards him.

Jack doesn't move.

"C'mon, Reynolds, let's not fuck about any longer."

Jack stares at him, his face immobile.

"Hand it over, okay, and we'll come to some arrangement. Something mutually beneficial."

"Hand what over, Tommy?" Jack's voice is calm and even, as if this were all some kind of picnic.

"Do me a favour, Reynolds. You honestly expect me to believe you came all this way out of the goodness of your heart? You know what she's looking for, and I'm guessing you've found it, cos you wouldn't be leaving otherwise, would you?"

I swivel my eyes towards the boat Jack unhitched. It's slowly drifting away from the island.

Jack regards him coolly, his steely gaze never wavering. He doesn't look at me once.

It's like I'm not here. Like I don't even exist.

"Come on, Jack," Tommy says. I try to turn to face him

but his fingers dig hard into my arm as he spins me back. "Stop pissing about. We all know what's going on here. You have something we want, something you want too. And there'll be plenty to go around, won't there? More than enough for everyone."

I see Jack considering this. Observe the indecision rippling across his face. Finally he nods, still not looking at me, and lowers the gun, tucking it into his jacket. A sharp intake of breath from the man behind me as Jack reaches with his other hand and withdraws Max's notes from his pocket.

"This what you're after?" he asks casually.

Something inside me dies as I watch him unfold the sheets of paper.

He's going to hand them over.

Of course he is. How could I ever have imagined otherwise? Those notes are Jack's passport to a better life. His freedom. His fortune.

And I led him right to them.

It's over, I know, as I see Jack scan the scrawl of Max's handwriting.

All over.

It's then Jack looks up, his eyes locking on mine. His left eyelid twitches, and he blinks slowly as if to chase it away. *Sorry,* his expression seems to say. *Sorry, Sarah, but really, what did you expect?*

I bite down on my bottom lip to stop myself crying, just as his mouth turns up into the hint of a smile.

"Hang on tight, Chicory."

Jack holds my gaze for a second longer before grasping the sheets of paper in both hands and ripping them in half. He clasps the pieces together and does it again. And again.

For several moments no one reacts as Jack reduces Max's notes to shreds, then tosses them into the air. The wind whips them up, scattering them across the lake like ragged white confetti.

"What the fu—" Tommy yells, but I never hear the rest. I'm shoved forwards as he lunges towards Jack, my head smacking against the rock as I fall. Everything goes dark, only for a second, then the shock of the freezing water jerks me back to myself. I try to struggle to my feet but there's nothing there. Nothing beneath me at all.

I attempt to swim upwards, to get a lungful of air, but as I surface I hear a splash behind me, then a pressure on my head, holding it down. Someone is pushing me under, I realize, and I have no strength left to fight him. A fire in my lungs begins to build and I'm seeing stars in front of my eyes, funny little lights that dance about like the jewels on the lake. Everything is swimming, fluid, and I have an odd sensation as if I'm coming round from an anaesthetic. Neither in this world nor the one waiting beneath.

"Sing," says a voice somewhere deep inside me, and I lose myself in the beauty of the music I can hear now all around me. I start to sing, clear in my head, reaching for the high note as the cold seeps into my bones, holding it pure and steady as the darkness creeps towards me.

And then it ends. A sudden, excruciating pain as someone grabs my hair and pulls me upwards. I surface with a gasp, a rasping breath that racks right through me, tears of agony mingling with the lake water streaming down my face.

Just to the side, at the edge of my vision, a man staggers onto the island, blood seeping from the side of his head.

Jack!

But no. Strong arms shove me to the shore. I grasp at the rocks and haul myself upwards, then hear a small *plish* as a bullet enters the water. I spin round. Over on the boat, a fair-haired man is aiming at Jack, getting ready to fire again.

"No!" I want to scream, but there's not enough air in my lungs. I'm seized by a violent fit of coughing and barely turn in time to see Jack falling into the water.

The breath freezes in my throat. *Oh god, no…*

I try to move, try to go back and save him, but my head is spinning and I haven't got the strength. All I can do is watch the surface of the water, waiting for the bloom of red that I know must come. I watch and wait, counting the seconds, until I'm sure he's gone.

"NO!" I cry, and this time it rings out across the lake, loud and sharp like the shriek of a gull. The man with the gun turns his gaze towards me. I'm dead, I think, as he lifts his arm and takes aim.

But at that second Jack surfaces and grabs the side of the boat, tipping it sideways. The man loses his balance and Jack heaves himself inside, grabbing the gun.

"Enough!" he yells, scrabbling to his feet and pointing the weapon at the fair-haired man sprawled across the bottom of the boat. Then swings it round at Tommy Crace, kneeling on the shore, his hand clutched to his head. The man who nearly drowned me.

"Enough!" Jack shouts again, his words resounding through the silence. "It's over!"

39

We watch the motorboat speed over the surface of the lake until it disappears round the curve of the bay. Overhead, billowy white clouds scud across the unending sky, the alchemy of the setting sun turning the water to pale gold.

Eventually even the sound of the motor wanes, leaving only the rustle of the wind through the reeds.

I shiver. My wet clothes cling to my skin, making me colder by the minute.

"What if they come back?" I ask, trying to stop my teeth chattering.

Jack sighs. "They won't. Tommy knows he'll be wasting his time."

"So it's really over?"

"For now," he nods. "For you."

Four words that tell me everything. I'm safe. They have no reason to come after me with Max's formula gone, lost in the bottom of the lake.

And I'm pretty sure there's nothing left of the drug itself. Because I think I know what Max did with it. And why.

But Jack. I realize he's not going to get off so lightly. Jack has betrayed them, and denied them a fortune.

Of course they're never going to leave it there.

I think of my brother, in the same situation, knowing the wolves were at his door, that there was no way to shake them off. He wasn't tough like Jack. He couldn't live with that, any more than he could live with what had happened to that girl. To Anna.

The note he wrote. It told me everything. That note was Max saying goodbye. His life was over, he believed, and he came here to die. He took what he had left of that drug, and it stopped his heart and by the time he was found, all trace of it had gone.

A wave of sadness ripples through me as I grieve for my brother. For the dead end he drove himself into. And Anna. What a waste. And I think of the damage to all our lives – Rob's university plans, Lizzie's ruined exams. My mother's breakdown.

And my missed audition, I realize, finally admitting to myself that I'm way too late.

Jack coughs, and glances out to where our boat drifts in the distance. I wipe my eyes, wondering why he let them take the motorboat, leaving us stranded here. How on earth are we going to get back before we freeze to death?

"The faster they leave, the safer we are," he says, reading my thoughts.

I scan the lake in every direction to see if there's anyone who might rescue us, but there's no sign of any other boats.

Only the ceaseless backdrop of trees and reeds, the occasional bobbing head of a water bird.

We're completely alone.

Jack stands and peels off his wet clothes, down to his underpants. His skin is almost blue with cold, but his body is tight and lean and I have to turn away before he catches me staring.

He lays his clothes out on the rock and I wonder what he's doing. There's no way they'll dry in this weather. It's nearly dusk and the air is turning cooler as the light disappears.

But Jack doesn't sit back down. Instead he goes to the edge of the island, peering into the dark water for a couple of seconds before diving in.

"Jack," I yell, jumping up in alarm, but he's already heading out towards the boat in a steady crawl.

Five minutes later, I see him pull himself over its side.

The moon rises slowly behind the island as we row away, at first a tinge of orange between the trees, then a looming white ball rising over them, astonishingly bright against the darkening sky.

I'm wrapped in the tarpaulin Jack found in the box at the back of the boat. He's rowing with the one oar we have left, using it like a paddle, first one side, then the other.

It's slow going, but at least we're moving. Jack doesn't

speak, just examines the play of the moonlight on the ripples as if hypnotized by the impossible beauty of it all. Out of nowhere, the wind drops, the water going as still and clear as glass, the silence so deep you could drown in it.

"Do you think it was a full moon then?" I ask quietly. "When Max…" I can't say it.

"Maybe," Jack says, lifting his eyes to the perfect sphere hanging above us. "It would be nice to think so."

He leans over and pulls something out of his jacket pocket. A glint of metal, dark and hard, then a splash as he drops the gun into the water. I imagine it sinking slowly into the depths of the lake, silt settling around it like a caress.

And then we catch the sound of voices, improbably near. The low dull hum of an outboard motor. Jack spins and looks around us.

"Is it them?" I whisper, holding my breath. "Are they back?"

"Shhhh…"

He holds the oar in mid-air, letting the boat drift. A fish flashes out of the water right to the side of us, making my heart leap. The sound of the motor draws nearer, and up ahead, in the distance, a boat slides into view. I can hear people talking in Swedish, a man's voice and a woman's, sounding far closer than they actually are.

We watch them glide past in the twilight, heading towards a group of islands further up the lake.

"Fishing."

Jack's voice has relief in it. I let myself breathe again as he carries on paddling the boat. Pretend to gaze out over the lake, but really I'm studying him out the corner of my eye. He's put his jeans back on, but his chest is bare and the muscles in his arms and stomach contract with each tug on the oar.

I want to ask him if he was tempted, when that man offered him a fortune.

But I don't need to. I know he was. And I know there's nothing to forgive him for. It's not wrong to hesitate in the face of temptation, I understand that now; what counts is having the strength to turn your back on it.

So instead I ask the question that's been playing around my head for so long I can't hold it in any more.

"You tried it, right?"

"What?"

"The stuff that Max made."

Jack looks straight at me and then averts his eyes. For a moment I think he's not going to answer.

"A few times."

"What was it like?"

He thinks for a while, contemplating the way the moonlight spills across the waves. "Amazing. At the time it made everything feel so…so significant. But being here, now, I can see that was nothing."

"Like a dream, you mean?"

"Like a shadow. Like a picture of something real. Like a

postcard from somewhere wonderful you can never go back to."

We fall silent for a while, listening to the suck and slosh of the oar in the water, following the moon as it rises higher in the evening sky.

Jack nods towards it. "There's so much beauty in the world, Sarah. You don't need pills. You only need to open your eyes."

My heart turns back to Max. Did he see this too? Did he come down to the lake to watch the moon before he…my mind shies away. Sorrow sweeps through me again with such force it feels as if it might just kill me.

"I'm lost," I say, my voice choking. "I don't understand anything."

Jack gazes back at me, and even in the dusk I can see the softness in his eyes.

"We all are, Chicory. That's the point. We're all dreaming and we don't know how to wake up."

I think of the nightmare I had last night. Max and me. Running. Terrified.

"I want to wake up," I whisper.

Jack smiles. "Not yet, Chicory. Not every dream is bad. You've got a whole lot of good ones ahead of you yet."

I lean back into the boat, letting my hand trail in the water, soft as silk despite the cold.

"Will you do something for me?" Jack asks.

"What?"

"Sing something."

I look at him. He's staring right at me. Is he serious?

"What? Now?"

He nods. "Your voice is lovely."

I sit up. "How do you know?"

He doesn't reply. Simply carries on rowing.

"You listened, didn't you? When you were following me?"

He doesn't confirm it, but it's there, in his face. He's gazing at me with such a solemn expression I don't have the heart to refuse. I pull the tarpaulin tighter around me and straighten my back. Hum the key to "Dido's Lament" for a minute, then lift my head and begin.

"*...on thy bosom let me rest...death is now a welcome guest...*"

As I sing the first lines from Purcell's aria, I hear my voice ring out over the lake, the water reflecting and amplifying the sound until it feels as if it's all around us, shrouding us with the loveliness of Dido's haunting expression of grief. And as everything drops away – the cold, the fear, the exhaustion – I know in the very depths of me that this is all I ever want to do.

The only time I feel truly whole.

"*...When I am laid, am laid in earth...*"

My eyes shift from the moon and settle on Jack. He's stopped rowing again, watching me, his mouth slightly open as he listens. I build to a crescendo and let my voice swoop and soar, let it dance on the waves and mingle with the moonlight, let it wash away everything until there's only the music.

"…*may my wrongs create, no trouble, no trouble in thy breast…remember me, remember me…*"

I gaze back towards the island and let the tears flow down my cheeks. I'm not singing now for Jack, nor for myself. I'm singing a requiem for Max, for my brother, for everything he lost, and for everything we lost when he left us. I'm singing for his life – and death – and putting all that I have left in me into the song.

"…*remember me, remember me, but, ah, forget my fate.*"

The last note lingers and dies in the night. Jack inhales and doesn't speak for ages. Then finally clears his throat.

"Never stop," he says, his voice jagged. "Promise me that, Chicory. Promise me you'll never stop singing. Not many things in life are worth a damn, but that…"

He breaks off and looks away.

I focus on my feet, trying not to cry.

"I want you to invite me." He turns back, fixing me with that slow, serious stare.

"Where?"

"To your first concert – when you're a famous…a famous…" I see him groping for the word. "…soprano."

I smile through my tears. I haven't the heart to tell him I'm an alto.

"Go home, Chicory. Forget all this. Leave it to your dreams. Just concentrate on your singing."

"It's too late," I say miserably.

Jack frowns. "Why?"

"I've missed the audition."

He looks at me intently.

"When was it?"

"This Saturday morning."

Jack goes quiet for a few minutes. I watch him calculating our chances of getting back in time.

He needn't bother. I've already added them up and made zero. Besides, there's no way I'm ready – not after all that's happened.

He takes a deep breath then sighs. "Don't think like that, Sarah. It's never too late, do you hear me? I'll come with you, talk to them if you want. Explain."

I laugh. The idea of Jack turning up at the Royal Music School, demanding they give me another chance, is so absurd that I have to.

Jack fixes my eyes with his. "There'll be other opportunities, okay? You're not your brother. You haven't screwed up like that."

I study his face, letting the truth of this sink in, and something lifts in my heart. He's right, I think. He's absolutely right.

This isn't the end at all.

friday 16th september

I find Jack standing down by the pavilion, gazing out over the lake. The sun has risen and there's a light mist on the horizon. A gang of birds swoops and wheels over the water just past the jetty.

I hand him a mug of tea. "There's no milk, but at least it's hot."

I'm shivering despite the blanket draped around my shoulders, but Jack hardly seems aware of the cold.

"We should go soon," he says.

I gaze at the lake, trying to imagine the sheet of ice that will cover it over in winter. In only a few months. It feels impossible, all this life, all this movement, frozen for weeks on end.

"Okay," I say, but suddenly the thought of leaving this place tugs at my heart so forcefully I'm tempted to refuse. Max, my brother, who lost his way and ended up here by himself.

How can I leave him alone?

In the distance I hear a long, low howl, fading back into silence. I sense Jack shiver beside me.

"Reckon it's a dog or a wolf?" He looks at me with his grey-sky eyes and all at once I understand what they remind me of. Wild and fierce and piercing.

And dangerous, I think, remembering the gun.

"What will you do?" I fix his gaze with mine, not letting it slide away. "When we get back, I mean."

Jack shrugs. Then seems to consider the question more carefully.

"I'm not sure. I've been thinking maybe I'll go travelling. I fancy Asia. Somewhere really different."

"What about college? You said you wanted to study horticulture."

He shrugs again. "It may have to wait."

I understand what Jack means. And why he needs to get away. I stand for what feels like ages, looking out at the lake, listening to the sound of the birds and the wind in the leaves. And I think of Phoebe, and how Jack won't be able to see her at all. He'll be in exile, like Lizzie, for who knows how long.

Though Lizzie can come home now, I realize. As soon as I get back I'll call her, tell her there's no longer anything to keep her away. And I know that everything will be fine between us.

She, at least, isn't lost to me.

"Jack," I say, turning to face him, "I need you to promise me something."

"What?"

I feel my cheeks colour. "Just swear to me you won't...

you know…touch that stuff…or get involved with it again. Ever."

He sets his mug on the little table in the pavilion and lifts his hand, placing it on my cheek.

"I won't, Sarah, I give you my word. I'm done with all that."

His hand lingers and I don't draw back. Those winter eyes pull me in, and then I feel his mouth on mine and with it a surge of longing that makes me giddy. I kiss him back, wanting to hold this embrace like a perfect note I never have to let go. I want to sink into it and never have to surface.

But Jack gently draws back and runs his hand through my hair. Then leans towards me again, this time resting his forehead against mine.

"This isn't the answer, Sarah." His voice soft and quiet. "This would just be the beginning of the problem."

I feel his words like the ground dropping out from underneath me.

"Jack, I…"

I want to say it. More than anything in the world I want to tell him what's in my heart. But something in his expression holds me back.

"Maybe one day, Chicory." He lifts my chin and looks into my eyes. "But don't hold your breath, okay?"

I pull away, biting my lip, blinking hard. I know he's right. I know I have to get on with my life.

But I never wanted more to be wrong.

I turn back, unable to meet his gaze. "Are you ever going to tell me why you call me Chicory?" I try for a smile, but don't quite make it.

He reaches out and puts his forefinger under the tip of my chin, forcing me to look up at him. "Eyes as blue as a chicory flower, and…"

He hesitates for a moment.

"And what?"

"…something of an acquired taste."

He grins, using his thumbs to wipe away the dampness from my cheeks. Pulls me to him in a hug so tight I can barely breathe.

Then releases me.

"I saw a restaurant right outside town on the way here. How about I take you there and treat you to a proper breakfast?"

I look at him, take a deep breath of the cool morning air, and finally manage to return his smile.

And realize, for the first time in a very long time, that I'm absolutely starving.

ACKNOWLEDGEMENTS

Many, many thanks to Sarah Stewart and her tireless editing of *Better Left Buried* – I bow to your persistence and dedication. Thanks also to everyone else at Usborne who contributed their time and encouragement – Rebecca Hill, Anne Finnis and Becky Walker. Also many thanks to my publicists Amy Dobson and Megan Graham, who have done their utmost to spread the word.

A special thanks to my agent, Jo Williamson, and for my beta readers, particularly the wonderful Wendy Storer. Also to everyone at YAT and Book Frisbees for their invaluable advice and support – you know who you are.

Thanks again, Chris Murray and Marie Adams for helping me keep my life in order. And an honorary mention for Stanley and Mrs Perkins, the best things on four legs.

Above all, much gratitude to James, chief beta, cook and crisis manager. Just couldn't do this without you.

ABOUT THE AUTHOR

EMMA HAUGHTON worked as a freelance journalist, writing features for a wide variety of newspapers and glossy magazines, before becoming an author. A mother of four, she now lives and writes fiction in Dorset. *Better Left Buried* is her second novel.

If you've enjoyed Sarah's journey, and would like to see pictures of the Swedish island or hear the pieces she sang, please follow the links at

www.emmahaughton.com

also by emma haughton

Inspired by a
true story

NOW
YOU SEE
ME...

...but can you trust me?

Emma Haughton

**NOMINATED FOR THE 2015
CARNEGIE MEDAL**

ISBN 9781409563693

Three years ago, thirteen-year-old Danny Geller vanished without trace.

His family and friends are still hanging on to every last shred of hope. Not knowing if he's alive or dead, their world is shrouded in shadows, secrets and suspicions.

This is the story of what happens when hope comes back to haunt you. When your desperation is used against you. When you search for the truth – but are too scared to accept the reality staring you in the face.

Because sometimes perhaps it's better to live in the dark.

"The novel bravely explores how it feels for those who are left when they simply don't know what happened."
The Independent on Sunday's
"Best books for children this Christmas"

"Perfect for anyone who enjoyed *Girl, Missing* by Sophie McKenzie." **Daisy Chain Book Reviews**

"A beautifully paced thriller which grips from its intriguing start to its unexpected and electrifying finish. An impressive and intelligent YA debut…"
Lancashire Evening Post

"Well-written and incredibly gripping."
theguardian.com children's book reviews

"A must-read for fans of a good thriller." **Book Angel**

if you liked BETTER LEFT BURIED,
you might also like…

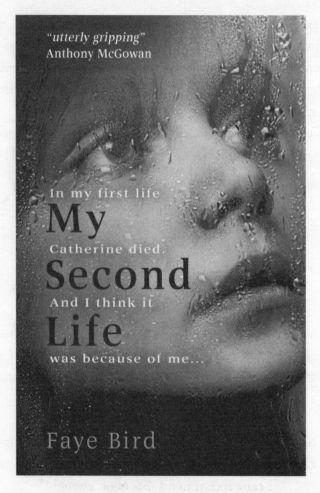

"utterly gripping"
Anthony McGowan

In my first life
My
Catherine died.
Second
And I think it
Life
was because of me…

Faye Bird

ISBN 9781409578604

"The first time I was born, I was Emma. I was beautiful. I had everything to live for. But I died. I was 22."

15-year-old Ana has always known that she's lived before, haunted by memories that aren't hers – memories of being Emma. But when her two lives collide in one chance meeting, suddenly she's bombarded with terrifying visions of a little girl who tragically drowned.

Was Emma responsible? Consumed by guilt, Ana will do anything to uncover the truth.

"This debut thriller gets off to a cracking start."
The Daily Mail

"A haunting debut that grips you from the outset."
The Bookseller

"An ingenious concept, an intriguing mystery and a gripping story told with pace and passion… An amazing and thrilling debut." **The Visitor**

"*My Second Life* is heartbreaking, heart-racing, has an amazing lead character and the story is like nothing I have read before. I can't recommend this book enough!"
Reading Away the Days

for more electrifying reads check out

www.usborne.com/youngadult